THE
HOUSE
OF
LITTLE
BONES

BEVERLEY LEE

Published by Ink Raven Press
Copyright © 2021 Beverley Lee

All rights reserved. This book or
any portion thereof may not be reproduced
or used in any manner whatsoever without
the express written permission of the publisher
except for the use of brief quotations in
a book review.

ISBN-13 978-0-9935490-5-2

Cover design by
ELDERLEMON DESIGN
Interior design by
PLATFORM HOUSE PUBLISHING

All books by this author

The Gabriel Davenport series
The Making of Gabriel Davenport
A Shining in the Shadows
The Purity of Crimson

The Ruin of Delicate Things
The House of Little Bones

Find out more about Beverley's work at
beverleylee.com

*For those waiting for
their chance to shine
and
for Luca – the bringer of light*

THURSDAY – DAVID

David Lansdown had always wondered what it took to break a man into little pieces. To peel away all the privileged layers of his life, to split him open until the true horror of what he was and what he had done became the only things he could cling to.

Five days ago, he would have laughed at the preposterous idea of it all. He would have said such things belonged in the pages of a book.

Five days? Was that all it had been? Tonight, he felt as if everything before those days existed in another lifetime. But not just the days—it was the nights. Oh God, those nights.

He pressed his palm against the thick pane of glass protecting him from the dark. Protecting him from whatever roamed the wild and desolate moorland beyond.

He had thought he was untouchable.

Behind him, stacked neatly on his desk and illuminated by the soft glow of an Anglepoise lamp, were the words he had typed. All of them since coming here. All of them really the self-narrative of a man flaying the skin of his past from his bones.

Any resemblance to actual persons—living or dead—events, or localities, is purely coincidental.

That was a lie. But what followed was the truth.

Sunday – David

five days earlier

It all started with a photo.

A lucky snap by a paparazzo crouched on the high wall surrounding the restaurant. The offending woman had risked life and limb by straddling the sharp metal wire topping the wall at the rear of the building. Had even probably come away with a few cuts or grazes. But it had been worth it. It rocketed the sleazy little online magazine she worked for into the stratosphere of the big boys and sealed the fate of his golden literary career.

It was such an innocent photo. The older man with winter-flecked hair styled messily but elegantly. Just a little too long. Just a little too rock star. His Savile Row jacket slung over one arm, his made-tomeasure jeans just a little too off-perfect. In the background the maître d' hovered, his form nearly eclipsed by a tall Christmas spruce tastefully decked in strings of fairy lights.

Most people waited months for a chance to dine in this most exclusive boutique hotel restaurant. The man had only booked a table a few hours before.

Because David Lansdown wasn't most people. He was one of Britain's most distinguished authors, a mantle he had worn around his shoulders like an ermine-capped cloak for nearly three decades.

That bloody photo. His hand resting protectively against the slim back. The upturned face to his, the golden glow from the lights illuminating the youthful jaw, full lips slightly open. Yes, it was obvious to anyone with an ounce of intelligence that David Lansdown and his young companion were a thing.

Maybe it wouldn't have been important if his companion had been just an ordinary person. But the adoring face turned to him belonged to Luca Carlyle Fox-Waite, the son of his lifelong best friend, Charles Montague Fox-Waite, CEO of the publishing house David came under.

In the list of Bad Decisions, his little dalliance with Luca came right at the fucking top, and it was why he found himself in the middle of nowhere on a sulky grey afternoon in February.

†

A piece of white paper stuck to the door of the house fluttered in the wind.

It was the first thing that caught his eye as he climbed out of the taxi into the mean winter light. That same wind caught at his scarf and sent it whipping over his face. David Lansdown swore under his breath, tugging his collar up against the arctic chill.

What had he expected? A welcoming committee?

No one here knew or, he suspected, cared who he was. There would be no more adoring fans walking past his fashionably unkempt Notting Hill home. No more instant recognition as he went about his daily life.

And it was all his fault. A triumphant middle-life crisis, the papers had said, but they didn't mean it kindly. In a few weeks he had managed to single-handedly destroy his whole life, and it was only by the grace of God and the fast, sweet-talking action of his agent that he'd managed to slither out of it with some shreds of his career left.

Having a relationship with the son of his best friend? Slightly outrageous. Having a relationship and keeping it secret until it exploded like a pus-filled cyst, making said best friend look a fool? Yeah, well, there aren't enough adjectives for that.

'You need to take yourself out of public view for a while, David,' Imelda Davros had said as they sat on a bench overlooking the South Bank. It was the middle of December, and the annual Christmas mayhem was in full swing. Twinkling lights dotted the barges slowly lumbering down the Thames, and from where they sat he could smell the hot, sweet scent of roasting chestnuts.

'David, listen.' Her sharp retort brought him miserably back to the present. 'Get out of London and write me something spectacular. I'm your agent, not a miracle worker, and the paparazzi are baying for your blood right now.' He could feel her cool, green-eyed gaze slicing through him. Imelda was the one person who saw through all of his bullshit. She had an unnerving knack of being right about everything, something David both loved and hated her for.

He paid the taxi driver in cash and grabbed his holdall from the boot. Everything else he required for his three-month stay had arrived yesterday, Imelda organising everything with her usual razor-sharp skill. Not that there was a lot; mainly boxes of books and paper copies of old manuscripts he liked to keep close.

And his desk. The one he had written every novel at.

Part of him had wanted to tell her he was more than capable of organising it himself, but instead he had taken off for the day and spent it licking his wounds at the back of a non-descript coffee bar.

David Lansdown, the UK's most successful horror writer, whose books constantly rocketed onto the *New York Times* Best Seller list, was living in his own horror story. But it wasn't filled with ghosts and haunted houses, it was filled with scandal and the frosting over of relations with his best friend.

Charles Fox-Waite wasn't stupid enough to oust him from the fold; David was too profitable for that, even though his last two novels hadn't quite gained the usual praise.

You know how this business goes, he'd told Charles as they sat at the bar in the Ritz, surrounded by the golden glow of art deco glamour. *Readers love a name they can trust. They'll come back.*

As he watched the taxi reverse and swing around, exhaust fumes ghosting in the frigid air, he wasn't so sure whether his words might come back to bite him.

And then he was alone, staring at what was to be his home for the next three months. Newly built, it was an architectural wonder of moorland stone and grey slate and limitless glass—so he'd been told—standing at the top of a flat-capped hill. The land it stood on had belonged to a local sheep farmer. When the old farmer died and his son inherited the farm, he did what his father had warned him never to do: He sold off the plot of land with the spectacular view. Imelda couldn't understand why no one had snapped up the house. Apparently the couple who commissioned it from one of the area's leading architects had only lived there for a month, citing unexplained occurrences for their rapid flight back to the city and leaving all their furnishings behind.

It's perfect for you, David. What horror writer doesn't want to live in a possessed house?

But now, standing outside in the failing light, with the black bones of winter trees hulking on the shoulder of the hill, he wondered whether he had come here to rebuild his life or to fade away into obscurity.

He ran his teeth over his lips and worried a small flap of skin until it split. The sharp sting cut into his morose thoughts as he crunched over the gravel pathway that led from the gate to the house.

He plucked the note from the door. It had been nailed there and the offending nail remained, a scar on the pale oak surface. He growled under his breath. If someone wanted to annoy him, they were going about it in the right way.

He stuffed it into his coat pocket without reading it and brought out the door key. As he slid it into the lock, he paused and turned around.

There were no other houses in view, just the rolling, desolate topography of the wild moor as far as the eye could see. The wind whistled around the eaves of the house as though it was furious something now stood in its way, and for one moment David was aware of his own insignificance in this particular landscape.

The smell of new paint loomed out of the darkness as he stepped inside. He fumbled for the light switch, his hands skimming over plastered walls, finding nothing.

Something creaked deep inside the gloom, and despite not believing in anything to do with the supernatural, his heart kicked up a gear. Behind the scent of the paint, he could smell something bitter and pungent in the cold air.

His fingers found the switch. Light flooded the house, and David caught sight of his new home for the first time.

The designer had created something extraordinary. David was well used to beautiful and aesthetically pleasing buildings; his inner circle was full of them. But this? This was something special. The open-plan ground floor consisted of a tasteful large living area with a wood-burning stove, the room decorated in shades of grey and cream. Reclaimed floorboards gleamed with a new wax coating, and from this rose an open-stepped wooden staircase leading to a glass-enclosed hallway to the first floor.

Through this David could see the stained-glass sunburst at the apex of the double-height windows Imelda had gushed about, which overlooked the rear of the property.

He let out a slow whistle of appreciation, and for the first time in a long while, felt a little of the tension slip from his shoulders.

David dropped his holdall and walked across to the kitchen area, tucked away to the left. It was small but very stylish, the cool grey units contrasting with the pale quartz countertops. A glass dish sat on the island worktop, a note slid under its base.

Happy new home shit, read the note, and he smiled. *There's wine and a microwave meal in the fridge, but you need to learn to cook. I'll be over on Saturday to see how you're settling in. Meanwhile, try and get some words done. I hear the neighbours are quiet!*

David could almost see Imelda's face as she'd scrawled the words, and he was suddenly very grateful for her towering presence in his fucked-up life.

He checked the cupboards and found one stacked with glasses. His hand was on the fridge door when a harsh scent wafted across towards him. He turned, inhaling until he found the source. Upstairs. He glanced up to the darkening wall of glass, dusk hovering like a wraith.

His footsteps echoed on the open treads as he walked slowly to the top, his eyes scanning the darkness. He flicked on the lamp, suddenly aware of the silence. He could hear himself breathing, and that one single observation shocked him. It seemed very wrong.

The walkway stretched out in front of him, leading to the bedroom. The vaulted wooden roof beams above formed a natural arch, and through an open door he could see the white-clad bed beyond. But his attention was drawn by a small dish on the floor directly beneath the stained-glass sunburst. Grey smoke wafted lazily from a small bundle tied together with cotton. A black feather rested on the floor next to the dish.

Carefully, he knelt and examined it further. White sage. He knew the connotations of burning this. To cleanse a space. To purify. To get rid of negative energy. It definitely didn't look like the kind of thing Imelda would have commissioned.

He picked it up and the heady smell made his eyes water. This was going right out of the door. He clattered down the stairs and marched across the floor, yanking open the door and tossing the bundle outside. As a second thought, he threw the dish out after it. It shattered onto the gravel, but his sense of satisfaction quickly evaporated.

It was so dark outside now he couldn't even see the bumpy track he'd driven in on. There were no streetlights to pierce the gloom. Nothing but the start of a long, long night. *But why should that matter?* He tamped down the sudden rush of anxiety. It was all because this was very new, and he wasn't comfortable in new. He liked the routine of familiar things and places. And this was as far from familiar as he could get.

This was his house for the next few months, whether he liked it or not, and he was standing here in his coat as though he didn't belong.

Annoyance grated at his nerve edges. Who the hell had lit the sage stick? And why?

He shrugged. Maybe it was some local trying to do him a favour after the hasty exit of the last owners? If so, they were wasting their time because it was all a steaming pile of excrement. He had paddled in the paranormal all of his life, and not once had it sunk in its claws.

He shook his head and stuffed his hands into his coat pockets, and found the note that had greeted him.

It had been torn from a small jotter, its top edge ragged with little holes. The writing was in capitals, in red ink, the letters heavy as though whoever had written it needed to make sure the words stuck.

ONLY ONE BELONGS HERE

Cryptic as fuck.

He tore the note into shreds and tossed it into the air. The wind gathered it up and swept it out into the night.

SUNDAY – DAVID

David stared at the flashing cursor on the document until his vision blurred. He'd typed a few pages and then lost his flow. His gaze flicked to the window.

Night had swallowed the horizon, thick blackness pressing against the glass. The moor was all but invisible, but he imagined it as dark and purpled like an old bruise. The sky above was too large and wild. Too all-seeing.

He went to the kitchen and poured himself a mug of coffee.

The prospect of maybe living here permanently flitted into his mind. He stood for a few moments trying to decode the numbness weighting his limbs. Trying to make it fit into a vague outline of a fledgling character. A character that was far too much like him.

He could write that man. Give him a new name and new responsibilities. Give him a new life.

An internal monologue began in his head as he opened the fridge and grabbed the fresh bottle of milk, his mind already cranked into working mode. But what fell from the bottle wasn't the easy flow of milk. It was thick, curdled globs. They dropped into his mug, then floated on the surface of his coffee in a nasty, greasy slime.

Disgust curled his upper lip. What the hell? He checked the date. It was days in advance.

A sharp ping interrupted his confusion. He threw the contents of his mug down the sink and checked his phone.

Have you eaten yet?

That was it. No fancy emoji, no wasted words. Imelda checking up on him, although sometimes he wondered if her care was based more on the commission he brought her than friendship.

The basic phone felt clumsy in his hand. Part of the deal he had made with Imelda was going a week without stewing in his own juices. She needed him focussed and creatively abundant, not dissecting the online tabloids for his own name, frittering away the day.

No internet. No car. Just an emergency means of communication if needed.

It would be strange having no broadband, but he'd lived without it before, back when he was new and fresh to the game, working three jobs and writing feverishly until the small hours.

Up here, there was no chance of him adding to his already sullied record. Regret over his actions lurched into his chest as he fired off a reply.

Not yet. Writing.

Imelda wouldn't expect anything but the briefest of exchanges. David uttered a satisfied *ha*, could almost see her raised, immaculate brow.

He returned to the screen, determination and more than a shake of pure stubbornness making his fingers fly across the keys.

A little while later he glanced down at his word count. A warm spike of achievement fizzed through his veins. This was more like it. A grin split his face and he laughed, the sound falling away like a stone in a well.

His stomach grumbled loudly and he realised he hadn't eaten anything but a dry, unpalatable shop-made sandwich before he'd left London.

He pushed back his chair and padded into the kitchen. The overhead lighting pulsed into life as he rounded the corner, the soft gleam of metal caught in its glow.

David grabbed a glass from the shelving over the sink and ran the cold tap for a few seconds. Air clunked in the pipes and he followed the sound with his eyes as it ran up the walls and disappeared. Leaving the glass under the tap, he opened the fridge and poked around in the stack of pre-cooked meal containers until one caught his eye.

Thank God for Imelda and her skill at ordering anything online, although the grocery van must have had a hell of a job finding the house.

He gave the plastic tray a shake, peeled back one corner of the film lid, and stuck it inside the microwave. Five minutes and he'd have a hearty beef casserole lovingly prepared by some gourmet company he had never heard of.

A gust of wind screamed around the roof, and for a moment he thought he felt the whole house tremble, which was impossible.

'Do not lose the plot, you son of a bitch,' he muttered, the line from one of his first novels, the one that had rocketed him onto the *New York Times* book list.

The trapped air suddenly cleared from the tap, and water vomited out, spraying the front of his shirt. He jumped back, the shock of the cold raising his heart rate a good few notches.

The flow spat a few times, then settled, filling the glass he'd placed in the sink. The water wasn't clear. It had a reddish tinge, like something rusty had dipped in a toe.

He looked at the glass, dumbfounded, as though staring at it would work some magic and it would clear before his eyes. Bringing it to his face, he sniffed it. It didn't smell of anything. He stuck the tip of his tongue in, rolling the taste around his mouth. It was just water, but with an odd iron-like edge. Maybe it came from an underground stream or a well? He made a mental note to check in with Imelda tomorrow.

But it had to be safe. The whole place had been checked before he'd moved in.

He shrugged his shoulders and gulped the water down, the chill easing the dryness lining his throat. The metallic taste lingered on his tongue for a few seconds and he smacked his lips. It was actually pretty good. If he'd still been in London, he could have marketed it to one of the floating bars on the Victoria Embankment.

He wondered when he'd ever walk those streets again. If maybe that part of his life was over and this was the start of a new phase. It was a very sobering thought, one that shocked the old David looking on.

The ping from the microwave burst into his thoughts.

Dumping the steaming contents into a bowl and grabbing a fork, he wandered into the living area. He'd not given it more than a cursory glance of approval when he arrived, but as he flopped down onto the grey velvet sofa, as he chewed the first mouthful of meat, he couldn't stop his thoughts from wandering to the great glass wall and ancient hills beyond.

His story could be out there waiting for him. He wouldn't even have to make up the bleakness; the atmosphere was there on a silver platter.

Forking another mouthful from the bowl, he decided that tomorrow he'd start to explore. A few hours' exercise in the fresh air would set him up nicely for a good, productive writing session.

He bit through something that wasn't meat. It slipped through his teeth and the sudden instinctual wrongness of it had him spitting it out onto his palm.

In the midst of a masticated heap of food lay the half-chewed remains of a cockroach.

SUNDAY – LUCA FOX-WAITE

Luca Fox-Waite sat in the park. He was chilled through, the wooden bench he'd been sitting on for nearly forty minutes anything but comfortable. He had his hands in his coat pockets, a beanie hat pulled down over his ears. His boots were covered in mud from the miles he had tramped.

It was close to dusk. A single lamp post light pulsed on and off at the edge of the path, as though trying to pierce the gloom was a task it wasn't relishing.

He should be at home, head down over his books. But since the news leaked out, all thoughts of his master's degree had fallen by the wayside.

Dark thoughts swirled in his mind; why the hell had he even come out here, anyway? A small laugh fell from his lips. Oh, that's right. It was supposed to be all about getting his head around the fact he'd been discarded like a piece of litter.

And probably to fume silently about a father who had expressly forbidden him to see David Lansdown ever again. But his father couldn't stop him from thinking about David.

His whole life seemed to be filled with men who treated his feelings as though they meant nothing.

He felt tied up in knots, threads unravelling from his perfect upbringing. But there wasn't much perfect about being a puppet in a house full of strings.

With a heavy sigh he eased himself up from the bench, feeling the blood rush into his feet and fingers.

By now, David would be far away at his new home.

He knew from overhearing his father on the phone to Imelda Davros that David would have no car and no internet. He'd be going cold turkey on everything but the most basic of communications.

He'd be settling down to write about demons and ghosts and unexplained things crouching in the gloom. It was a source of dark amusement to Luca that David had never encountered anything remotely paranormal, unless Luca considered himself a part of that.

As a child, no one had ever believed him. That the monsters were real. That sometimes he felt as if they lived within his shadow.

As he walked towards the park gate, as blackness hovered like a skulking dog, Luca let his thoughts drift back to the night they first came to visit.

He was six years old. The noise from his parents' party below echoed through the floor. The muted sounds of music. People laughing.

It was New Year's Eve and the weather decided to welcome in another year with an arctic blast of cold and driving rain. Against his window it lashed, roaring its rage, forcing its cold tongue through the gaps in the Georgian sash windows.

Luca couldn't sleep. He tiptoed to the door, stuffed lion in his hand. His sister, Lissy, had given it to him, told him it was so he could learn to be brave and fierce.

He opened his bedroom door a little, needing the warm light of the hallway. But someone had turned it off and only darkness waited.

A whimper left his throat. He wasn't tall enough to reach the switch. And Lissy's room was at the end of the hallway. He clutched the lion to his chest and tried to summon up the courage to walk into the gloom.

A stair creaked below, and there was the sound of heavy steps. If this was his father come to check on him, he'd be reprimanded for being out of bed.

Luca scooted back into his room.

The gap between his mattress and the thick carpet looked different tonight. He imagined he could see a shape curled within it, something dead, half-rotted. Something waiting for him.

He launched himself into bed, where the duvet lay twisted from his restless attempts at sleep. His head hit his pillow as the steps sounded in the hallway. His leg slid under the duvet as he frantically tried to untangle it. Luca closed his eyes tight.

And then he felt something cold and wet, like a dead fish, enclosing his ankle.

A cry burst from his lips as he kicked away the duvet, expecting to see a monster. His bladder let go and warm urine soaked his pyjamas and sheets.

'For God's sake, Luca.' His father entered the room, his shadow reaching Luca first. 'Get into the bathroom and clean yourself up.'

Luca slid out of bed, his wet pyjama bottoms clinging to his legs. As he shut the door to his bathroom, he climbed onto the plastic step and pulled on the cord to switch on the light.

He could hear his father on the phone, knew he was ringing their maid to come and change the sheets. Someone else to avoid looking at in the next few days.

As he fumbled with the tap to turn on the hot water, he tried not to look at his reflection in the mirror. Monsters lived there at night, everyone knew that.

He pulled off his wet clothes and stood there shivering as he washed himself down with a flannel.

But his eyes widened when they reached his ankle.

Where he'd felt the cold and slimy touch—of something he fervently hoped was a part of the duvet that had been towards the window and the winter chill—was a long, pink blister.

It didn't hurt until he looked at it. He pressed his fingers along the pocket of shiny skin. There was liquid underneath. The tip of his tongue protruded from his lips. He pressed a little harder. One edge gave under the pressure and the liquid squirted out, hitting him on the cheek.

This time he screamed, and this is where Charles Fox-Waite found his son, naked and inconsolable, as the clock ticked over into a new year.

SUNDAY – CHARLES FOX-WAITE

Charles Fox-Waite went to the window of his study and stared out at the landscaped gardens, backlit by strands of lights threaded through the trees. The bulk of the laurel hedge loomed at the bottom of the garden, the open archway in its centre leading to his wife's rose garden beyond.

It was a picture-perfect scene of all the good things in life, created by money and privilege.

But everything has a price.

He'd learned that many years ago. He'd been eighteen, fresh-faced and energetic, desperate for any experience that would make the blood surge in his veins. David had been an unknown author, busily penning his first book in the small hours as he worked three part-time jobs to keep a roof over his head.

A smile quirked on Charles's lips as the images outside blurred and memory took him back to that place. Sometimes it felt as if it had only been yesterday.

They'd stood at the bottom of the long, overgrown gravel drive, the hulk of the abandoned building just visible through the fog.

'This ought to do it, right?' David turned to him, his coat collar pulled up against the cruel November night.

Charles let out a long exhale, his breath hanging clouds of vapour. 'You want to go in there, the old asylum?' He fixed David with a look he hoped showed leadership and incredulity, but David was already unfastening the links of the chain wrapped around the huge wrought-iron gates.

'Why not?' David said as he slipped inside. 'You're not too chicken, are you?'

And, of course, that was that. David knew exactly how to play him.

They walked slowly up the drive, drifts of fog wafting across from the thick band of trees surrounding the ruined building.

Haught House was its name, but locals knew it as Haunt House. In its heyday it had been renowned as a place to cure the criminally insane, but documentation uncovered after its demise showed most of its inmates became noticeably more unhinged the longer they were there.

As they stood before its boarded-up windows with their

hanging slats, the brickwork covered in creeping ivy, Charles could well imagine what had gone on beyond its doors. The whole place just felt wrong.

He glanced across to David, saw his friend's mouth slightly open, his eyes shining with excitement and awe. And that's when he knew David would become a writer of extraordinary perception.

'Come on.' David was across at one of the ground-floor windows. Only one wooden board barred entrance, and it gave easily under David's tug. He clambered over and Charles heard his feet hit the concrete floor.

A beam of bright light hit his face. He squinted against its glare, and he heard David laugh softly. Knew if they actually found something that could be counted as supernatural, David would be over the moon. That's where they differed. Back then, David lived for the thrill of the shadows and the things science couldn't explain, whereas he had his feet firmly on solid, factual ground. Or so he thought.

The torch light dropped and Charles saw it sweep across the inside. David whistled through his teeth. 'Come and see, this place is amazing. The whole floor has collapsed . . .' His voice tailed off as he disappeared from the window.

'Fuck.' Charles swore softly under his breath and hopped onto the sill, despite the prickling doubt in his pores.

It took a few moments for his eyes to adjust to the gloom. It was the smell that overpowered him at first, mouldering wood and plaster, the dense green of rotting vegetation. Ivy hung in long trails from the ceiling and from somewhere came the sound of dripping water.

David crouched in the centre of the room, a huge void before him. Slabs of crumbled concrete clung to the edge as though something had chewed them apart.

'For God's sake, be careful,' Charles hissed, half imagining the floor collapsing, taking David with it.

But David seemed oblivious to the danger. 'Look, it's a tunnel. Runs all the way under the ground.' His torch swung across in an arc, the light eaten by the darkness below. He scrabbled sideways and peered over the edge. 'There's a ladder. Someone's been here before us.'

Charles wondered if that someone had never really left, but he kept that thought to himself. David was going down that ladder. And if he didn't want to be left alone up here, he was going down too.

He wasn't ashamed to whisper a small prayer as he descended, but the rungs were sound, albeit a bit slippery. David stood at the bottom, suppressed energy coiled within him. He thrust a small torch into Charles's hand the moment his feet touched the tunnel floor. Because that's what it was, a long, arched subterranean tunnel which seemed to run the entire distance of the house. It was built from bricks, the colour of old blood, the floor spattered with puddles of water from the dripping roof.

David ran his torch light across it. 'This is definitely going in the new book,' he said. 'The atmosphere here is on point.'

A chilled breeze wafted from somewhere and ruffled Charles's hair, the sound amplified from the tunnel walls.

'Which way do you want to go?'

'What?' Charles turned to face his friend.

'Which way?' David grinned. 'Left or right? I want to explore by myself, get a hold of the feel of this place, commit it to memory. You know, all that writer stuff.'

Charles could think of nothing more ridiculous than splitting up, but he wasn't about to say so.

'Fifteen minutes,' he said. 'We'll meet back here in fifteen.'

David nodded and was already striding away into the darkness, the brave light of his torch bouncing to and fro.

Charles blew out a breath through his lips and contemplated just waiting here for fifteen minutes. David would never know, but part of him felt an intense curiosity to just wander for a little while.

He set off towards the right, making sure he went in a straight line as there were secondary, much smaller tunnels leading from the main one. He shone his torch inside one. Something glinted in its beam.

Carefully, he edged towards the mouth of that tunnel. Its roof was only about six feet high and the rough-hewn stone it was constructed from appeared older than the main tunnel.

But the glint of something farther in made him curious. Cold stung his face, and the stench of wet green and old stone curled into his nostrils. The dripping was more obvious here too. More insistent in the close-knit confines.

The shape in the gloom grew more evident. The glint of a metal frame, decayed fabric hanging from it like flayed skin. Two large wheels still clung to the frame, along with two smaller ones at odd angles at its front.

An abandoned wheelchair.

A shiver rushed over Charles's skin.

Beside the wheelchair was an alcove hewn from the stone. A rusted iron door stood forlornly open, the top latticed with framework.

A cell.

Now he had to see what was inside, some kind of fervour leading him onwards, David forgotten.

He ran his fingers over the door, felt the freezing metal, rough under his touch.

The cell was very small, barely large enough for an adult to lie down in. It was empty apart from a hole in the floor at the back corner. A latrine. Charles wrinkled his nose.

He thought about a person being locked up here in the

dark. If they weren't unhinged to begin with, they soon would be.

He reached out and pulled the cell door closed, tried to imagine the terror of those forced inside.

The dripping water suddenly ceased, the silence cloying against his ears. Then he heard the breeze that swept through the main tunnel change direction and funnel down towards him.

Impossible.

But on the breeze came something else, a faint whispering. A voice repeating words over and over again at a rapid rate.

The breeze died.

The whisper did too.

Charles stood in the sudden silence, his face against the cold bars.

His heart thudded against his ribcage.

And then his breath caught in his throat as the hair in the nape of his neck rose.

Something behind him exhaled, the stench of it rotted and fly-blown. He pushed against the door, fear trip-hammering through his veins. It didn't move. He rattled it, his fingers curled desperately around the bars.

Words galloped through his head in a frenzy. Let me out, let me out, I'll give anything . . .

He felt the presence of something pressed close against his spine but couldn't bring himself to turn his head to look. A feeling took hold of his stomach. A slithering, as though something was inside him, crawling around his vital organs. Marking them as fodder. He stood, frozen stock-still in the dark, a terrified wreck of a man. For one brief moment, he understood insanity.

Give me something, *urged a whisper against his ear.* Give me something precious.

Yes, yes, *he agreed.* Anything.

The cell door flew open. It yanked out of his hands, left them raw and stinging. He bolted like a greyhound from a gate, knocking over the wheelchair in his haste.

The sound of its creaking, spinning back wheel followed him as he fled.

Back towards the ladder, back towards surety and logic.

Minutes later, he saw the bouncing beam of David's torch coming towards him.

'See any bogey men?' Charles kept his voice as level as he could.

'Nah, nothing but dust and shadows, my friend. Nothing but dust and shadows.'

And as they climbed the ladder to the upper floor, Charles thought about mentioning what he'd felt.

But something stopped him.

He didn't want David to know, because David would drag him back down to the cell and make him live through it all over again.

Sunday – Luca

Luca couldn't shake the claws of the memory. Even when he was back inside the warmth of the fashionable Kensington residence the Fox-Waites called home, it clung to his skin, as though in resurrection he had given it a new strength.

He passed through the entrance hall, climbed the wide, carpeted stairs. A winter floral arrangement sat on the round marble table, all perfectly classic of course, if a little indulgent. His mother was nothing if not fastidious in her taste. Allegra Fox-Waite chose everything well, and that included the marriage to his father. How much love was involved, Luca was never sure.

Luca paused at the turn in the wide stairs, glanced down at his great-grandfather's coat of arms on the wall.

Vivamus, moriendum est. Let us live since we must die.

Heaviness cloaked his shoulders. Sometimes it all caught up with him. The constant striving for success. The unattainable search for happiness. As though that were some kind of Holy Grail, and if you worked hard enough then all of its riches would pour down on you.

His laptop sat on his bed. He fired it up and punched in the area David had moved to. Sitting cross-legged, Luca scrolled through pages of links, lost in the black hole of search engines for well over an hour.

He was about to give up when an old web page caught his eye. Blocks of text in eye-watering colours sat on a pale grey background. The details at the bottom said it was last updated in 1998. But the area it covered was the closest he had found. It was a rambler's page with articles on the various footpaths and public bridleways that criss-crossed the moor.

His eyes scanned the screaming red text on one of the blocks.

> The first village we came to was Ashford, with its old church and older graveyard. There is an Iron Age ditch within the church grounds, and when they extended the church they found a bunch

of Anglo-Saxon bones and it's now a recognised ancient monument.

The route along the river isn't very well marked, but if you keep to the edge you eventually come across a stile where the path forks both ways. Take the left-hand one and that leads you up along the Four Peaks Way, where you have a glorious view of the valley below. Met an old guy and his dog and we got talking about the region. Out of the blue he told me that this area was where a young girl drowned a few hundred years ago. That her mother still haunts this place looking for her. Like he was trying to warn me. But more than likely he was hoping I'd scuttle off home.

Luca paused and chewed the edge of his lower lip. He pulled out his phone and shot off a quick text to David before he chickened out.

He grimaced when he noticed that he'd ended the text far too intimately, wanting to appear like it was perfectly fine that things were all over between them, but hey, that didn't mean they couldn't be friends, when it really was as far from fucking perfectly fine as it could be. Luca knew, despite everything, that he was still in love with David.

And that was something he would just have to work through in his own time.

His eyes scanned down the page and found another line of text near the end of the article.

> Had lunch at the local pub. Excellent faire. Found out from the bar maid that the locals call Four Peaks Way "the Coffin Walk."

Luca half thought of messaging David again, but Lissy knocked on his door telling him it was time for supper.

**TEXT MESSAGE ONE FROM LUCA
– UNOPENED**

Hey David, you probably don't want to hear from me but I've been doing a bit of digging on the area you're in. I found some old folklore about it, thought it might be of some use in your writing as you don't have internet right now. Let me know if you want it.
Luca x

Monday – Luca

Luca awoke with a start in the small, dark hours.

Something icy cold had touched his face. He pulled the duvet up to his chin, blinking away the shroud of sleep. His fingers went to his cheek. Why did his dreams feel so real?

His curtains billowed in a stiff breeze. He could hear dried leaves skittering around the patio below his bedroom. He didn't remember opening his window.

The small nightlight plugged into a socket by his bed cast a soft amber glow over the floor. Only Lissy knew about it. It was enough to keep back the night.

With a growl he rolled out of bed and padded across the room to close the window. He stood for a moment and gazed out at the manicured garden, at the perfectly clipped hedges. From here he could see his father's study. A light burned in the window.

It was 2 a.m.

He turned, lifted the duvet to climb back into the warmth. Dark spots dotted the pristine white sheet.

Luca flicked on the light and felt a flutter of alarm in his gut.

Blood.

His brow creased as he checked his arms, patted his face.

But it was only when he pulled up the legs of his flannel pyjamas that he saw what had caused it.

The mark on his ankle, from that terrifying New Year's night, was raised and inflamed. A fresh blister had formed over its surface and traces of watery blood dribbled down his heel.

Disgust wrinkled his nose along with a not-quite-awake confusion. Had he caught it on something?

But all he'd been doing was sleeping.

No one had ever investigated how the mark had come to be there. His father dismissed his questions, told him he must have knocked it while playing. His mother, as always, deferred to her husband.

Only Lissy had tried to come up with a reason. But back then she was only four years old, and her logic came down to pixies, that they had done it because Luca had made them cross.

So Luca had lived with it, and he had not been bothered by its presence except for the odd times when it itched and burned and he had to wear gloves to stop himself making it bleed while he slept. Maybe that's what he'd done tonight? But his fingernails were clean.

And now his thoughts were all too wired to sleep.

He pulled his laptop from the floor and opened the lid.

His searching took him from link to link, bouncing about until it settled on a small piece in a local newspaper.

City Couple Flee Haunted House on the Hill

But the article was only clickbait. Underneath were just a few paragraphs saying 'unexplained occurrences' had happened in the house and that they'd left for 'personal reasons'.

In other words, they refused to talk but the reporter needed something.

Luca popped across to Zoopla and found the house under Luxury Listings. It had an eye-watering monthly charge and was marked LET BY NETTLEFIELD AND LANE.

But the thing that interested him was that the couple had barely been there for a month.

Chewing his lip, he picked up his phone and sent another text to David.

The latter part he had found last night, but he stopped himself sending it as two texts in one day sounded a bit obsessive and he was frantically trying to keep it calm and friendly.

Then he looked at the time and groaned.

5:15 a.m. Now that did look desperate.

**TEXT MESSAGE TWO FROM LUCA
– UNOPENED**

Hey, me again. I hope you've still got this number. The couple who built that house you're in, they only stayed for a month. Pretty weird, huh? Anyway, I found the nearest village to you and did some digging about. Turns out they hold a yearly 'Burning', an ancient ceremony where pyres are lit on the moor, something to do with appeasing an old spirit. Thought it might be useful. Luca xx

Monday – David

Early morning fog clung to the hollows on the moorland, an ocean of mist covering the wild bracken and grasses like the tongue of a spectral god.

David Lansdown had slept fitfully. He'd woken at just gone 3 a.m., freezing cold, and despite hauling the throw from the sofa to his bed and pulling on a pair of socks, he couldn't get warm. And despite cleaning his teeth five times he still thought he could taste something unspeakable on his tongue.

He longed to be out of his front door and onto a street where people bustled past, where traffic stopped him from crossing the road until he took his life in his hands and cut between the throng of cars and buses. Where the barista in the coffee shop on the corner had his order ready as soon as he reached the till.

It was 8 a.m. and he was fully dressed. The length of the day yawned before him. A gust of wind howled across the roof, rattling the slates, whistling its way into the valley. The prospect of a day alone filled him with the kind of dread he normally inflicted on his characters.

He hadn't expected the solitude to be so draining. Hadn't expected to feel the sense of isolation so soon.

He filled the kettle and set it to boil, watching as the steam began to curl from its spout.

Regret took hold of his mind and shook it between merciless teeth. He had thought he was invincible, that he could have anything he wanted. And when his eyes had fallen on Luca during the party for his last release, he realised Luca was no longer the little boy he'd taken to museums, no longer the teenager who had hovered awkwardly on the outskirts at family gatherings. He was all grown up. And available.

Common sense should have told him to back away before his fingers got burnt, but lust has a habit of trampling over every other feeling with iron-clad hooves.

They'd been very careful, only venturing out together to public places with ties to Charles Fox-Waite's business interests. David had even teased the press with the possibility of a new lover, found on his last tour of the States, and they had clamoured for more but all he had given them was a boyish wink and that old-school charm he was known for.

No one even suspected that he was sleeping with the son of his oldest friend.

The steam licked the white-tiled wall and David watched as droplets of moisture formed on its surface then trickled away.

And now here he was. An old dog licking his wounds, a victim of his own ridiculous ego, his career in shreds.

He had rarely been in love, had managed to navigate the minefield of it, sidestepping most advances. It was all too messy, too time-consuming. His thoughts needed to be on his goals.

Until the child who continually earned his father's ire had grown up and tempted David just a little bit too much for him to resist.

David found himself caring a lot about what happened to the rich boy who existed on the periphery of his father's anger and expectations. He often wondered why Luca had made such an impression and came to the conclusion that if Luca needed saving maybe he was the one to do it.

Although David had never told Luca that he loved him, it was there so often on the brink of his actions. Luca never badgered him about it. Never demanded those three little words. He had always just been happy being in David's company.

He blew out a breath. Maybe Imelda was right. Locking himself away to concentrate on work was the only way to free himself of Luca's shadow.

He placed his hands on the edge of the Belfast sink and lowered his head, fighting the urge to scream his frustration into the silence. But deep down, he knew that his every action had placed him here, and the only person to blame was himself.

While he waited for his tea to brew he went back upstairs to retrieve the notes he'd made on his story last night.

The phone sat on his nightstand. A red light pulsed in one corner. Two text messages. From Luca. One from last night, one from early morning. David hadn't checked his phone before bed, resolutely trying to wean himself off the magnetic pull.

Some part of him wanted to open them. But he had promised Imelda he wouldn't. And besides, if he didn't reply Luca would lose interest eventually.

He tried to tell himself that Luca had only been a dalliance. A pretty young thing, just like all the other pretty young things he had left crushed in his wake.

He's better off without you, the sensible part of his brain chided him.

But a yearning still churned for the boy he had dumped unceremoniously when that photo leaked out.

†

An hour later he found himself swaddled in layers of clothing, watching the fog as it cleared in patches over the deserted moor. The sky was a brilliant blue, with the only clouds clinging to the distant hills. Two red kites circled far above him, their silhouettes caught against a watery winter sun.

He stood behind the house looking at the view he'd seen only from the tall windows. Mile upon mile of purple and grey, rolling across a landscape unchanged for hundreds of years.

In the far distance he could just make out the tiny dots of other secluded homes amidst the patchwork fields of farms.

He set off along the track that led past the house, the grass-tufted ground springy under his feet.

The wind blew at his back, buffeting him forwards, forcing its way through the fabric of his scarf. For the first time in many years he had no idea where his steps were leading.

The track began to climb slightly, veering to the left, and his eyes watered as the gusts blasted against the side of his face. Over the rise, the ground fell quickly, a drystone wall cutting across the middle of what he thought might be a glacial trough. Sheep huddled by it for warmth, but none raised their faces to watch him pass. He shivered, pausing to glance behind him.

He couldn't see his house. A sobering thought flitted across his mind. If he got lost out here, no one would come looking for him. His hand curled around the solid shape of his phone, safe in his pocket. His only link to the twenty-first century.

At the other side of the wall he could see the track as it meandered sideways up the hill. An old stone watchtower sat at the top of its sloping shoulder.

The sound of a dog yapping made him turn. A small white shape darted into the heather.

Someone was watching him from the top of the rise. A figure, a woman, dressed in a bright yellow oilskin coat and a deerstalker cap. He narrowed his eyes. A shooting stick hung over the woman's arm.

He raised his hand in greeting, but she didn't return his acknowledgement.

He shrugged, turning his back on her, strangely stung she'd ignored him.

David made the decision that he would walk up to the watchtower and then go back. Wandering about the moor without a compass was asking for trouble, and God only knew he didn't need any more of that.

DISGRACED WRITER FOUND DEAD ON MOORLAND. He could see the headline in his mind's eye already.

The sheep scattered as he reached the drystone wall, heaving himself over the old, irregular stones with a grunt. His feet landed with a loud squelch, thick mud oozing up over what he had thought were sensible walking shoes. He kept the grey shape of the ruin in his line of vision as he began to climb again, his thighs burning with exertion.

Thirst thickened his tongue and he lambasted himself for not bringing any water.

He reached the tower and ducked under the lintel, the door long since gone. The wind, which had been his constant companion, dropped instantly. In the sky above, a single kite circled, its cry piercing the silence.

David ran his fingers over the weather-pocked walls. Fronds of lichen clung to its mortar, tufts of coarse moorland grass growing at its base. He trailed his fingers along until he met the small open window. From here he could see his house, standing sentinel over the moor, sunlight winking from the glass. He could also see the narrow, worn path that ran past the house, carved into the earth, compressed by hundreds of weary feet over hundreds of years.

He remembered what Imelda had told him as they'd sat on the bench a whole lifetime ago. She had chosen this place for him, not only because of its remoteness but because of the folklore associated with it.

'Bring out your dead,' he whispered.

David Lansdown did not believe in anything supernatural. His feet were firmly planted in the world of science and reason. But that didn't mean he couldn't use it.

He stood for a few minutes more, then set off back down the hill, his eyes firmly fixed on the old Corpse Road.

The Bone Crone

Tick-tock.

Tick-tock.

The sound of time passing.

The sound of seasons blending and rotating, fresh shoots sleeping under their blanket of earth, leaf buds forming on naked branches. The cycle of life.

This year, she had slumbered fitfully, cocooned in her bed of dirt. Things had disturbed that place in the land where her feet had last touched it.

Not for her the sweetness of dreamless sleep. Of a peaceful transition to another place.

She had not known, when she swore her oath, what it would mean. How she would be tied to the land she had once walked upon.

She was too naïve, too undone with grief.

Too wracked with the need to avenge.

Her dead flesh had long since been a feast for worms. But curses lay in bones. They do not die.

Old Mother, they called her in the village. *Old Mother, how are you this morn?* they would call as they passed, raising a hand, doffing caps, children hiding behind their mothers' skirts. Because the young knew. They always did.

And she would nod in reply, her bent knuckles red and raw, pressing through her parchment skin as though they wanted to be free of their fleshy prison.

The Bone Crone, they called her in private. In their dwellings around their smoky fires they told stories of how she had sold her soul to the devil to live forever. In the taverns they laughed and used her name as a wager—*Five coins and the luck of the Bone Crone*—as dice tumbled on ale-sticky tables. All because she gathered those she could find, stacked them outside her shack and along the edges of the Corpse Road.

But behind every mention of whatever name they called her, the reasoning was the same.

Fear.

But they did not have to fear her then. She was simply an anomaly, an old woman who should have died decades ago, but who seemed oblivious to disease and the turning of the years.

They should not have feared her then, but they feared her at the end.

Her shadow moves now through this swathe of land. Hidden within every winter mist. Cloaked in the twilight of Novembers. It wears the mantle of the deep forests, blesses the feral spirits and the rolling wildness of the moors.

Everything that dies here feels her touch.

Something has disturbed the place where the coffin stone stood. Something has moved that stone away from the ground upon which it had always sat, weathering the centuries and all who passed. This ancient pathway, scored into the land, violated.

Something has disturbed her bones.

Something has disturbed her daughter's bones.

This last she cannot forgive.

And now she stands by the watchtower, drawn to the only thing that has not changed. Sees the blight on the landscape, the howling wrongness of its presence.

She knows what she must do.

Monday – Luca

When Luca went down for breakfast, his mother and father were already there.

'Where's Lissy?' he asked, and then his gaze swept across to her seat. He saw the used coffee cup and the toast crumbs on her plate. His heart sank. He'd forgotten she'd taken the first flight to Paris.

Breakfast as the sole junior Fox-Waite was always a struggle.

'What time did you get in?' His father lowered his newspaper a fraction.

Cold grey eyes met his. An arch of a pale brow.

The question sounded like an accusation.

'Luca didn't go out after supper.' His mother spoke up before he could answer, her eyes never leaving her planner.

Luca helped himself to coffee, bewildered as to why his father was suddenly so interested in his social life.

He wondered if his father was looking for any more scandal about him and David, but that was probably the domain of what Charles called the gutter press. There was plenty still circling online, you just had to know where to look. What they wrote had been twisted out of all proportion, moulded into something sordid and unclean. It was nothing like what he and David had. Used to have.

And despite being ditched like he had the plague when it all exploded, Luca still cared. He often wondered if they could have continued seeing each other if David hadn't been so well-known. But really, it was all down to what the affair had done to the Fox-Waite name and the reputation of the publishing house.

He let his spoon clatter into the saucer because he knew it annoyed his father.

In the back of his mind rose the fact he only had to survive two more years under his father's roof. Once his trust fund matured he would have the means to get his own place, and once he had his degree under his belt he could work anywhere. If he never wanted to see his father again, he wouldn't have to.

And then what would he do? Gather expensive objects to put in a penthouse flat. Entertain friends who maybe only gave him the time of day because of the doors he could open for them. It was a miserable reason for existence.

Or maybe he needed to take a leaf out of Lissy's book and stop worrying about other people. Just be himself, and if others didn't like it, it was their loss.

But the truth was that pleasing other people was engrained in his psyche, yet another trait that didn't fit into the Fox-Waite ethos.

He absentmindedly rubbed his ankle against the chair leg to try to rid himself of a sudden itch, and winced.

His mother gave him an odd look, lipstick perfectly applied even at this time in the morning. Luca suddenly felt as though the room was closing in on him. He pushed back his chair, excused himself.

As he reached the hallway his father's voice rang out.

'There's something seriously amiss with that boy.'

Monday – Luca

Luca went back to his room. He checked his phone. Nothing from David.

A little twinge of anxiety poked him in the ribs.

He hadn't expected a long-winded reply, but he had expected something, even a terse thank you.

There was something about what he had uncovered so far that didn't feel right. David once teased him that he had a sixth sense, but Luca knew David didn't believe in anything like that.

An idea crossed his mind. Luca picked up his phone and called Lissy, hoping she was free to answer. If she couldn't talk, she'd always call back as soon as she could.

He listened to the dial tone, imagined it ringing out in some Parisian hotel.

'Hey, Luca.' Her voice, the one that always made him feel safe. 'Are you okay?'

It was testament to how much of a train wreck his life was when this was the first thing she thought to ask.

'Yeah, I'm good.' Luca opened his laptop. 'Do you remember telling me about that woman, the paranormal researcher you wanted to pitch a book to you? The one who refused.'

There was a short silence at the other end of the phone. He imagined her flicking through the vast mental data base of everyone she knew.

'Olivia Taverner?'

'That's the one.' Luca knew that was her name but he didn't want to alarm Lissy by making things seem too . . . *What? Urgent, intense?*

'She definitely wasn't interested though. Shame, really. That house she lives in has so many stories. Why do you ask?'

'Do you still have her details? I'm trying to find something out and I'd rather get information that I know is sound and not hearsay.'

'For your dissertation?'

Luca paused. 'No, for something I'm trying to find out for David. Something I left unfinished.'

He hated lying to her, but if she thought something was wrong she'd be on the next plane back.

'Are you two talking again?'

This is what he loved about Lissy. There were no recriminations, no 'You shouldn't be doing this, what the hell are you thinking?'

'Not like that. I'm just trying to help him with some folklore research. Can you shoot me her direct email or number, Liss?'

'She's not the kind of woman to waste time on people she doesn't know. I'd try email first, that way you won't be on the cutting edge of her tongue.'

'Ah, I'm kinda used to that,' Luca said with a wry smile.

'Sorry, Luca, I need to go. Have a meeting in the office with some new author who's supposed to be the next big thing. I'll send her details as soon as I can.'

She hung up and Luca sat for a while just cradling his phone in his hand. What Lissy did was exactly what his father wanted him to do, but he had no appetite for being a cog in the Fox-Waite Empire.

His father had been catastrophically angry when Luca told him that he wanted to study folklore. It was one of the few times Luca had stuck to his guns, although his father hadn't spoken to him for weeks afterwards. Luca guessed it was because he didn't believe in anything that couldn't be scientifically proven, that he thought Luca was wasting his time learning about things that didn't exist.

Sometimes even Luca wasn't sure what had drawn him to it. Maybe because he wasn't brave enough to throw himself into a full study of the supernatural, as that always seemed too near and this was as close as he wanted to get.

He remembered David asking him a question about the Danish celebration of Saint John's Eve. About the burning of those modern wicker men. The night David had walked with him to the rose garden and they'd both suddenly become tongue tied.

The night David first kissed him.

The phone pinged. A slow smile touched his lips.

His email to Olivia was very polite, offering Lissy's name by way of introduction and then the area he was curious about. He mentioned his field of interest and asked for verification of the local tales he had already found, and any supernatural occurrences over the years, ending with gratitude for Olivia's time.

As he pressed Send he wondered if it would even be read, let alone answered. But at least he had tried.

Olivia's answer came as he idly flicked through what he was supposed to be doing for his dissertation. He was way behind in his planned timeline for submission, but he knew he couldn't concentrate on anything else until he had sorted out the things that were bothering him about the area David was in.

A little voice told him he was only using this as an excuse, a reason to still be in contact with the man who had dumped him. Luca contemplated that he might have masochistic tendencies.

He opened the email and let the words sink in, speed reading first, then going back to pick up the details.

His heart felt like it was doing things a heart shouldn't do.

Area rife with supernatural sightings going back to the 1600s. Grid reference you gave me is interesting, as it appears in many of these possible haunts.

Folklore also very evident but, as you know, it's a very difficult thing to pin down as any truths may be lost through word of mouth or misinterpretation. I can confirm that the burning ceremony you mentioned goes back to around the same time as the first supernatural sightings.

The house that now stands on the grid reference, the place the locals call Bone Hollow, is the first erected dwelling space there, despite its prime location.

Luca swallowed the moisture that had built up in his throat.

Bone Hollow. Why is it called Bone Hollow?

He shot off a quick reply, thanking her and asking for any more information if and when she found it.

Another email hit his inbox.

I hope this isn't to do with your sister trying to wheedle her way into my interest again?

Luca grimaced, could almost feel the ice hidden behind the words.

He replied by assuring her that wasn't the case, and that his interest was only of an academic nature. He hoped she didn't think he was grovelling.

The definition of insanity is doing something over and over and getting the same result, so when Luca had refreshed his inbox multiple times in a ten-minute period to no avail, he finally gave up and padded downstairs. The house was quiet. Relief flooded through him.

He was edgy and full of energy, and thought that maybe he'd go for a run in the park. But as he passed his father's study on his way to the kitchen for a bottle of water, he noticed the door was slightly ajar.

He slipped in and closed it softly after him.

It wasn't a welcoming place, despite being full of books. Sunlight speared through the sash window, highlighting his father's huge mahogany desk, which was supposed to have been used by Charles Dickens at one point.

All Luca could remember were the times he had been sent for, standing before this desk with his heart hammering as his father finished a phone call or a letter.

The times his father made him sweat.

He fixed his gaze on a small burn in the Indian rug by the desk. What he'd always done when he was waiting. Felt his thoughts turn inward.

Theirs was a proud and important family, Luca would be told, and there were expectations to be met. Luca should think more before he acted, realise the repercussions on the family name.

He should be more like his sister.

Alice Cordelia Fox-Waite was younger by two years, but Luca always thought she was wise beyond her age, or maybe that was because she had learned to navigate the minefield of Fox-Waite life while he felt like his whole existence had been peppered with shrapnel.

Luca and Lissy, together against the world. They had written that on the sand during every family holiday. Watched as the waves carried their bravery away into the depths of the ocean.

Luca blew out a breath through his lips and gave himself a stern talking to. He wasn't a kid anymore.

And the reason for being here—even more so than the fact his father would be horrified—was to search through his father's extensive library of books into the occult and the unexplained. Charles Fox-Waite's beliefs were the same as David's. These things couldn't exist. But he was more than happy to make a healthy living out of them. And having his own library only added to his draw when agents or writers came to visit.

The ticking of the Victorian carriage clock on the mantle rattled against the raw edges of his nerves.

Luca wasn't even sure where to begin searching. He ran his fingers over the spines, pulling a few out to glance through, then discarding them. In the bookcase behind his father's desk were the hardback first editions of all the writers in his publishing stable. Luca could see the bold font used in David's name, pride of place on the top shelf.

He edged towards them. Something hard dug into the sole of his foot. On the floor was a very small key, almost lost in the pattern on the Indian rug.

He picked it up, let it sit on his palm. The sun disappeared behind a dark cloud and the room dimmed.

Luca wasn't sure there was anything in this room that warranted a key. His father would never think anyone would dare to enter his hallowed space without his permission.

He scanned the shelves. Scanned the room with its wood panelling. His gaze lit upon the desk.

With a glance towards the door, Luca circled it. None of the drawers had a keyhole.

He twisted his mouth to one side, half wondering if the key was to something not in the room. Then he saw the other desk tucked away in the far corner, bought as an antique, not something to use.

Polished yew with a sloping lid hinged at the back. Cabriole legs with button-shaped feet. A Davenport desk. A writer's desk. The side contained four drawers, and it was these drawers that drew Luca's attention.

The top one had a keyhole.

He slipped the key into the tiny hole, his heart hammering wildly.

The drawer slid out reluctantly, as though it didn't want anyone to see what was inside.

Something wrapped in black velvet.

Luca unfolded two corners and found himself staring at the side of an oblong box. The edges were stained and tattered. The smell arising from it made him wrinkle his nose.

He almost dropped the box in surprise as what it was met his eyes.

Locked away in Charles Fox-Waite's study, the man who publicly declared that the supernatural only occurred in books, was a Ouija board.

†

After putting the board back into the drawer, being very careful to fold the cloth in the same way, Luca left the key exactly where he'd found it.

He left the study with too many thoughts bounding around his head. It's not as if he could ask his father why he had it.

His logic tried to make a modicum of sense. Maybe it was some kind of book promotion tool? There were always odd things arriving at the house. But none of them were ever hidden.

No, this was something with its own secrets.

Luca knew his father wasn't quite the upright pillar of society most people saw. From conversations with Lissy he knew Charles Fox-Waite would snuff out any perceived threat to his publishing empire. But this?

He checked his phone, had an intense urge to mail Olivia and ask why someone would have a Ouija board hidden away.

Now that he knew it was there he didn't like the feel of it. His skin prickled.

The silence of the house ticked against his mind. The air felt wrong. Too heavy. Too thick.

He changed into his running gear, both to get out of the house and to give himself something else to focus on. Out into the thin daylight of a February afternoon, the trees bereft of leaves, the cold wind chafing against his bare legs.

Run, Luca, run, that insistent voice told him, and for a moment he didn't think it was talking about the here and now.

He crossed the street. Jogged down past the aloof houses with brand new cars sitting in the driveway, over the main road where a bus blared its horn as he darted in front of it, into the park, all open and green, despite its location.

He could breathe again.

The park was mainly empty save for a few people walking dogs and parents forced out into the chill by hyperactive toddlers. He ran down the main path, then veered off to the right, to the narrow, almost circular track that led past the pond.

Bone Hollow. The rhythm of it drummed in time with his heartbeat.

Up the hill and over the Japanese bridge, the rush of water on rocks below his feet. Past the children's playground.

Sweat ran down his spine and he could hear his breathing hard against his ears. But he was in the zone now, that zone that cut away all other thought, his feet finding their own direction.

It wasn't until he reached the stone archway at the other end of the park that he realised where he was heading.

Up the steep hill, flanked by high stone walls, the narrow pavements forcing him onto the road at some points. Cars flashed by.

He dug in and powered up the last hundred metres.

In through the black iron gate, past the silent gatehouse. Into the land of stone and silence and bones.

His phone vibrated against his arm pouch. He read the text as he walked around in a circle, his heart rate pounding in his ears.

> If you need to talk, you know where I am. Lissy xx

He wished she was here. She could tell him he was being an idiot for getting so tied up in knots over the jittery feeling that things were far from right.

Luca silently asked for permission before placing his hands against a Celtic cross. As he stretched out his calf muscles, his gaze fell on the inscription etched into the stone. Below the names and dates of the family buried there something much more ominous met his eyes.

All that is left is bone and memory.

Luca wiped his hand across his mouth as the failing light hovered over the cemetery. He was suddenly aware he might be the only thing breathing in this place of the dead.

Bone Hollow. The name rattled against his mind again. Each time, he liked it less and less.

He thought about the Ouija board in his father's study, of David living in a place tainted by the past. And as he retraced his steps down towards the park, walking quickly as the cold settled against his skin, part of him wanted to turn away from whatever pathway this was leading him on.

Monday – David

At some point in the afternoon it had started to rain. David lit all the lamps in the house, but still, it seemed as if a shadow of night lurked in the unlit corners. He told himself not to be so bloody skittish.

When he found the first patch of water under the stained-glass window, it did not improve his mood. But he couldn't work out where it had come from. The whole glass window wall had no openings and he couldn't see any signs of water damage on the vaulted ceiling. He mopped it up with a tea towel, making a mental note to check it out in better light.

Supper was another microwave meal, which he poked through carefully before eating.

Rain blasted against the windows and the wind howled around the eaves. He put another log into the burner, cranked up the thermostat, and settled down on the sofa with a book and a glass of wine, his feet resting on the coffee table.

It was a striking design. A huge natural-edge oak slice sat atop an oblong of pitted old stone. Not quite to his taste, but all the furniture had been left by the previous owners. Some part of him wondered why they departed so quickly, if he should be worried about irate locals brandishing pitchforks outside his door.

He put down his book and ran his fingers along the rough sides of the stone. It felt just like the old watchtower, cold and mournful. Something forgotten.

When he settled down again he put his feet up on the sofa.

With the sound of the rain hammering down and the log burner crackling, it should have been the perfect atmosphere for relaxation. Yet he found himself reading the same sentence over and over again. It was the new release from Abigail Patrick, a writer he admitted, albeit begrudgingly, to be an up-and-coming new light in the publishing world. There was a freshness about her writing that hadn't yet been crushed. If he was truthful, he guessed he was a little jealous.

David gave up after an hour, drained his wine glass, and headed up to bed, pausing at the spot where the water had been. It was only then he realised that it was the same place where he'd found the burning sage.

He laid in bed listening to the rain. Usually the sound calmed him, lulled his senses into a place of comfort and security, but tonight there was no contentment to be found. He tossed and turned, unable to find the string which would mercifully pull him into sleep.

But as it always must, exhaustion finally took hold, spinning him away into darkness.

†

The sharp noise yanked him from the tangles of a dream. He sat bolt upright in bed, felt the iciness of the room against his sweat-slicked skin.

He listened, straining his ears against the silence, but all was quiet. Even the rain had stopped.

Reaching across to the bedside table, he flicked on the lamp. The brave glow seemed to barely make a dent in the darkness.

David padded out of the bedroom, stared out of the huge expanse of glass, wondering if what he'd heard had been out there. Just as he'd convinced himself that the noise had been in his imagination, something caught the moonlight streaming through the window.

Tiny fragments of glass lay strewn over the walkway, glittering like diamonds.

Carefully, he edged towards them, saw the lampshade sitting askew.

The bulb had blown.

It had blown without even being lit.

Tuesday – Luca

When Luca went down for breakfast his father was the only person at the table. Luca had slept too late after spending the evening creating a file with everything he had learned so far about Bone Hollow. He would give it an extra day to see if anything else turned up, then print it out and mail it to David the old-fashioned way.

He needed David to read it, to take heed, and he wasn't sure where this need was coming from or why it was so strong.

To find his father sitting in the dining room sent his mood plummeting.

'Luca.' His father carefully folded the newspaper and laid it on the table. 'Have you any plans?'

Luca felt his jaw drop open. He tried for extra seconds to answer by reaching for the coffee pot. His father never spoke to him like this.

'I'll probably work on some research,' he finally blurted out. Well, that wasn't a lie.

'Good idea. Keep your head down and forget about anything social for a while.'

Luca felt his father's grey eyes studying him, but he pretended to be oblivious as he poured a dish of cereal.

'About David.'

Luca paused with the spoon halfway to his mouth, waited for another blast of disapproval.

'He's very settled where he is. He's in a good space, and the new book is underway.'

'You've spoken to him?' Luca asked before shovelling the cereal into his mouth. It tasted like dust on his tongue.

'Yes, many times. He won't be coming back.'

Luca swallowed, or tried to swallow. His muscles had forgotten that movement and the sludge slid painfully down his throat.

He wasn't sure what hurt the most, that his father had spoken to David while David ignored all of his texts, or the fact his father appeared to be sure David wasn't returning.

'Best to concentrate on what's right for you now, Luca. Ignore any well-meaning friends and get the work done. Forget the outside world.'

With that, his father pushed his chair back, picked up the newspaper, and left.

Luca stared at the coffee pot. At the way the polished silver reflected his face, twisting it all out of proportion.

For a moment when his father had started talking, it seemed as if he'd had a glimmer of interest in Luca's life. But it had all been a front, a way to pave the way to deliver yet another blow.

He wondered why his father hated him so much.

†

Luca tried to fill his day with other things.

He cleared out the stack of old uni work in his closet, then walked to the end of the street and sat at a table at the back of his favourite coffee shop, watching other people hulked over laptops, meeting friends.

The buzz settled his nerves a little, but he still felt out of kilter, as though something was trying to tear him from this reality and plunge him into something unknown and infinitely terrible.

Fuck you, Father, for yet again holding a metaphorical knife to my throat.

He mused that if his throat was cut his father would deny all responsibility, stating he was merely holding the knife.

'Luca!' A voice shattered his internal monologue.

He looked up and met the eyes of the girl at the counter, her glasses half-fogged in the steamy heat. He saw the unspoken words waiting to pour forth.

He pointed to his phone, placed it against his ear, then swept past the girl. 'Hey, Anushree, how you doing? Just need to take this.'

He opened the door and went out into the freezing cold, making a show of having a conversation. Everyone knew that Rise 'n Grind had the worst signal in London.

When she had her back turned, he quickly made himself scarce. He felt bad for deserting her, but one thing he didn't need now was sympathy, and he knew Anushree had that in abundance.

He returned to the house, where he felt he both should and shouldn't be.

†

Luca's phone vibrated just as he was finishing supper. His father was out with a client so it was only his mother's eyes that met his.

'Sorry,' he said, almost on autopilot. Phones were not permitted at the table in the Fox-Waite household.

He desperately wanted to see if it was from David.

Maybe it was something about the way he could hardly keep his hand away from his pocket, or possibly a sliver of maternal fondness forcing its way through her impeccable presence, which made her wave him away as she placed her napkin onto her plate.

He shot out of the room before she could change her mind, but he didn't look at his phone until he was safely inside his room with the door shut.

It wasn't from David.

But his despondency at this was saved from hitting rock bottom by the fact that it was from Olivia.

Village census records a woman named only as Mary—not of the village but 'of Bone Hollow'. Found it interesting why they made a point of separating her.

And later, in parish records. Mary of the Moor—convicted of 'the gossip of women' (which could just mean she did something they disagreed with), banished from the village, May 1637.

Of course, this may not be the same person. Mary was a common name. But 'of the moor' has me thinking that she lived out there, which was rare, as pockets of civilisation stayed together for safety if nothing else.

Luca sat back, curling his lower lip under his teeth as he thought.

Why would they banish her instead of the usual punishments? And the answer came back as clearly as if she was whispering against his ear.

They be afeared.

He wheeled around, felt the chill behind him. His blister began to itch.

There was truth out there on the moor. He could sense it, all the pieces floating around inside his head, a puzzle just waiting to deliver its message.

And he knew, more than anything, that David was in a dangerous place.

Tuesday – David

The ping from the text pulled him out of a restless sleep. Imelda.

He groaned and focussed his eyes on the blurry message.

> I need words, David.

Outside it wasn't quite light. He rolled over and tried to go back to sleep, but an insistent throb in his bladder made him roll out of bed and head to the bathroom.

As he rinsed his hands he raised his head and grimaced at his shadowy reflection in the mirror. Bedhead hair and dark stubble. Eye bags to match. He leaned forwards and opened his mouth, moving it from side to side to see if the eye bags disappeared.

Sheer fucking vanity. He was fifty years old, and if all life had given him was this he should count himself lucky.

Behind him he could see the stained-glass sunburst on the window. Moonlight illuminated each panel, making the glass look as if it were lit from within.

Padding across the floor, he went to the glass wall. The full moon hung over the shoulder of the hill, the dark hulk of the watchtower silhouetted against it. Thousands of stars bore witness just as they had done for thousands of years. *Luca loves the constellations, can name each one.* He drew in a breath at the sheer beauty and wildness of the scene right outside his door.

Maybe he should just stay up. Make coffee. Watch the dawn break.

Fragments of glass littered the floor from the exploded bulb. He carefully inched around them, creeping down the stairs, felt the oddness of a strange place against his skin. As he reached the last one something caught his eye on the coffee table.

With lips pursed he stood and looked at the small object for a few moments before picking it up.

It was about an inch in length, off-white in colour. He turned it over in his palm, telling himself it couldn't be what he knew it was.

A finger bone. A finger bone that hadn't been there the night before.

†

David tried to come up with a logical reason for the bone, but the best thing he could think of unnerved him more than a little.

Someone else must have a key. Maybe they were the ones who lit the sage. Imelda might not have had time to change the locks, or she could have thought that wasn't necessary. After all, he was the only house for miles, and he wasn't exactly on a burglar's prime route.

But the thought of someone prowling around while he slept left an unpleasant taste on his tongue. He hadn't bothered to bolt the door last night. Tonight, he would.

When he looked back on it all it seemed this moment was when he should have left. Screw what Imelda might say. The benefit of hindsight. If he'd known then what he knew now, things would be so different.

He'd be a changed man, not a broken one with this terrifying guilt notched against his heart.

He didn't deserve Luca. He never had.

He found a spare light bulb in a cupboard and swept up the glass, ignoring the little voice in his head that kept asking how an unlit bulb could explode.

Then he threw himself into his writing, although he hadn't expected it to flow so well with the spectre of the bone hanging over him. He made a note on his pad and circled it. *Spectre of the Bone—title?*

On more than one occasion he forgot that he didn't have broadband when he wanted to fact-check. It was so easy these days, everything at your fingertips. The whole world available at the click of a button.

Everything comes too easy.

Another doodle in the margin. *Appreciation? Have we lost the meaning?*

It was only the silence messing with his mind.

He fumbled in his desk drawer and found an ancient Sony Walkman. The batteries were corroded to hell, but after a bit of scraping and finding new ones in a kitchen drawer David was more than surprised when the tape already inserted began to play. The poignant sound of Ultravox's *Vienna* filled his ears.

The music soothed his tattered nerves as his fingers flew over the laptop keys. He'd always written quickly, but this time it felt as if his words couldn't wait to be penned.

When the lamp on his desk went out, he had a moment of peculiar disorientation when the music continued to play.

Late afternoon had crept up like a thief in the night and the house lay in layers of shadow. He did that weird thing people do when there's a power cut— he tried to flick on a light.

He had the presence of mind to press Save on his Word document just in case.

But he didn't have a bloody clue if this place had any emergency candles.

David sat in the gloom for a few moments and contemplated his next move. So, no power. This place was far too remote to be on the National Grid, so it must have a generator. He vaguely remembered Imelda mentioning it had one in an outbuilding, but of course he hadn't taken much notice. That's the problem of privileged living, you never think the things you take for granted will stop working.

Muttering under his breath, David donned a jacket, grabbed a torch he found under the sink, and headed out into the rapidly falling dusk.

The wind took his breath away as he stepped outside. It was the kind of wind that burrowed its way under any flaps of clothing, the kind that contained freezing pellets of hail.

David struggled around to the side of the house where he'd noticed the log store on the day he'd arrived. Behind it, he could just make out the square shape of some kind of out building.

A loud bang made him wheel, his heart catapulting into his throat. The wind had caught the door and sent it careering back against the wall, leaving the house open to the elements. He wondered whether he should go back and shut it, and decided not to.

The door to the outhouse was held together by a wing and a prayer, but sure enough inside stood the squat metal shape of the generator. It didn't have any lights on.

David swore under his breath and was just about to press a few buttons when the dark suddenly became less so. He glanced over his shoulder and felt the heady rush of relief.

The harsh glare of the security light flooded the pathway, its beam reaching to the gate and slightly beyond.

He turned, thought he saw a hunched shape. A hunched shape on the Corpse Road. But when he looked again it was gone

Now, as he thought back, it seemed like a warning.

As he walked back to the house, the gravel crunching under his feet, head bowed against the cruel wind, the hairs on the nape of his neck rose.

But he put it down to the rain running under his collar.

The human brain will always try the logical conclusion first.

TUESDAY – DAVID

Another night looming. Another lonely pile of carbs in a plastic tray.

Imelda had stocked the fridge with all kinds of healthy stuff, but David found the thought of cooking for one too much of a hassle. In London he ate out most of the time.

As he stirred the contents of his bowl of chicken and rice with his fork he found himself listening to the sounds of the house: The incessant patter of the rain against the windows. The low whir of the fridge-freezer. The occasional throaty roar as the boiler kicked in when the temperature fell.

He'd told Imelda he didn't need his TV or any other form of distraction. He'd said it proudly and still remembered the glow of satisfaction in his chest.

But what he called confidence was simply arrogance wearing a different skin.

Now, he would have given anything for what his father had called 'visual wallpaper' sitting in the corner. Just to listen to another human voice.

He mentally chastised himself as he shovelled another forkful into his mouth.

Three days and you're already drowning in self-pity. Get a fucking grip!

On autopilot, he picked up his phone. Luca's unopened texts stared back. Part of him wanted to open them, to reply, but Imelda would wipe the floor with him if she found out.

Not to mention what Charles would do.

David couldn't afford to burn any more bridges.

It wouldn't surprise him to find out Charles had started monitoring Luca's phone. For someone who annoyed him as much as Luca, Charles seemed to keep him on a very tight rein.

David rolled his shoulders back and let the fork clatter back into the bowl. Okay, time to stop the moping and write.

As he walked to the kitchen, his gaze flicked to the door. Tonight the deadbolts were fastened.

After dumping the bowl in the sink he poured a

glass of red wine. Already, his mind was on the story and where it would take him tonight.

The lamp at the top of the stairs was lit. He could see its reflection in the glass on the window wall, a small golden pocket of warmth against the deep, yawning blackness. The track of light travelled almost halfway down the stairs, fading with each tread.

A frown lined his face.

There was something on the treads, something shimmering.

He went to investigate, taking a gulp of wine as he wandered towards it, sure it must be a trick of the light.

He knelt and ran his hand along where the illumination hit the stairs.

His fingers came away wet.

David paused, his gaze fixed on the wet patches.

He rolled his tongue around his mouth.

He looked up at the vaulted ceiling.

There must be a leak with all of this god-awful weather. But part of him wasn't so sure.

He had a sudden flash of memory of a horror film he'd once watched, where a creature from a swamp terrorised a group of teenagers. It had left wet patches in its wake and, as all good horror monsters do, had picked off the kids one by one as they went to investigate the strange noises outside.

His soft laugh fell into the stillness, but he heard the uneasy edge it carried.

As he mopped up the water his gaze strayed to the dark landscape beyond the window.

Running across this land was the Corpse Road where, for hundreds of years, the dead had made their final journey from the tiny hamlets dotting the moor.

Dead that maybe met a terrible end through illness or assault. It wasn't hard to imagine restless spirits wandering the landscape, searching for a way home.

In all of his long years of research and writing he had never come across anything supernatural, even though he had stayed the night in haunted houses and wandered alone through midnight graveyards. If anything did exist, it had decided to leave him alone.

Until now.

As he fired up his laptop and read over what he'd written earlier, that thought stayed with him until the words began to flow.

†

It was just before midnight when his dry and itching eyes forced him to abandon his work. He drained his glass, grabbed a glass of water, and headed up the stairs.

As he came to the lamp he reached to switch it off and paused. No, tonight he'd leave it on, just in case he needed to come down for more water.

But he knew that wasn't the real reason.

An odd smell met him as he went into the bedroom. He sniffed, trying to decipher what it was. It was musty, almost earthy, and for the second time that night he felt the hairs rise along his skin.

He investigated the bathroom, but all was fine. It was definitely coming from the bedroom, but he couldn't pinpoint the source.

As he slipped his toothbrush back into its stand, his gaze went to the mirror. David saw the tension corded along his neck, the worry etched into his brow. He bowed his head.

And then a sound made his head jerk up.

A *drip, drip, drip*. But it wasn't coming from any of the taps.

It was coming from within the walls.

†

David climbed into bed and pulled the duvet close. The lamp on the nightstand was off, although he'd deliberated leaving it on.

He remembered Luca used to have night terrors a lot when he was a child. They'd started after a New Year's Eve party when Charles had returned from upstairs, his face pale and drawn. It took three months for Luca to trust David enough to tell him what had happened that night.

One evening in high summer, they'd been sitting on a sand bank watching the setting sun liquefy as it fell into the ocean. Luca laid his head on David's shoulder, his skin glowing with a touch of too much sun, and David could still recall Luca's scent, a warm, clean musk with a hint of citrus from his sunscreen.

'It felt real, you know, when it was happening.' Luca closed his eyes for a moment, and David turned his face to kiss his brow. 'It still feels real if I think about it too much.'

Luca had believed. He still believed, and for the first time, lying here in the dark, David understood the abject fear of being afraid of something you don't understand.

Something that defies explanation.

The first time Luca sleepwalked, they were staying at a cottage David had rented in the Dales. It was close to Eyam, the village infamous for cutting itself off during the plague of 1666, thus condemning its inhabitants. David wanted to get a feel for the place and take some research photos for his next project.

The tiny thatched cottage stood next to the churchyard and they'd spent an afternoon wandering through the weathered stones, enjoying the fact no one gave them a second glance.

By supper time Luca started to feel nauseous. His head hurt and he'd told David it was a migraine. David fussed over him, packing him off to bed and waiting until the pain pills had kicked in.

A line from one of his recent books had come back to him. A character discussing psychic abilities with a sceptic. Empathy with the dead can take many forms. One of the most common is a migraine, for the lifeless can only speak through pain.

He shook his head at fiction poking its way into his reality.

†

In the middle of the night David awoke suddenly. The space beside him on the bed was empty, moonlight lacing across the wall.

'Luca?'

The name fell into the stillness. He loved the sound of it on his tongue, how the second syllable vibrated in his throat.

David rolled out of bed and padded to the window, sweeping aside the curtain.

There, by the moss-coated wall of the graveyard stood Luca. He was naked, the moonlight turning his lithe body to marble.

David watched him for a moment, entranced, before common sense rushed in and he grabbed the throw on the chair and ran down the stairs.

He didn't think any locals would be out walking in the middle of the night. But he was trying to keep his relationship with Luca under wraps and didn't want anyone rocking the cosy little boat they had built.

He half expected to meet Luca on his way back. But Luca hadn't moved from the same spot.

It was only when Luca didn't respond to his name that David understood. He slid the throw gently over Luca's shoulders, his gaze flicking to the dark gloom of the churchyard. Pale stones and the uneasy sleep of the dead.

The phrase settled in his mind, butterfly soft.

David led Luca back into the cottage, back upstairs into their bed.

He remembered the surge of protective feeling as he lay awake, waiting until Luca's breath had settled into the easy rhythm of deep sleep.

And now he lay alone in another bed, his heart thudding unnaturally quickly, his palms sweating, before finally drifting off into a slumber filled with something that wanted to drown him in the dark.

WEDNESDAY – LUCA

Luca climbed into bed just after midnight. He'd updated the file he was going to send to David in the morning, had written two texts with words he hoped David would read.

He sent the first one. The other stayed in drafts ready to send tomorrow, because he couldn't send two. That pathetic spurned lover thing.

He'd tried to keep his words casual, really wanting to spill all his fears that *something* didn't feel right. But David would only shake his head. And more than likely think Luca was getting more desperate for a reply. Which was the truth, but not in the way David thought.

Luca wondered if the voice he had heard earlier *had* been a figment of his own imagination.

His head spun with all the whys and hows, uncertainty a tentacled mass sucking all the logic from his brain.

He closed his eyes and exhaustion plunged him deep into darkness.

†

Something cold and doughy took him by the hand. It pulled him forwards, and in the way of dreams, everything fell away, tumbling sideways like a toppling domino wall.

A bitter wind stung his skin and he looked down at his body. He was naked apart from a string of small bones around his neck. They rattled together as he moved, following what led him through a thick, churning mist. Moisture droplets trickled down his skin, settling on his lashes. Through the mist he heard the cry of birds, a mournful, piercing call that made his scalp tighten.

A voice called his name and he turned his head, saw a circle of sunlight off to his left, like a stage spotlight in a pitch-black theatre. Lissy sat on a single chair. She clutched a piece of paper to her chest.

The scene shifted and Lissy was still there, but she was a little girl, her feet swinging over the side of the chair. Luca reached out for her. The bones around his neck clattered together as if in anger.

He tried to speak but couldn't move his lips. The fingers of his free hand moved languidly to them, felt the threads looping through and over.

Lips sewn shut.

Silenced.

As Lissy's image wavered like a heat haze over a desert, she held the piece of paper out to him.

A single word.

Stay.

And then she was gone, lost in his dreamscape. He heard a young girl scream, a sound that amplified his own terror. And then something appeared through the shifting gloom.

Something tall and solid. He knew this shape . . .

He was pulled skywards. Flickering candles floated past his vision.

The hand leading him fell away.

A stomach-churning lurch as he dropped like a stone, the rush of raging water close by.

Didn't you die if you died in your dreams?

A bone-jarring jolt—and his eyes flew open.

He was on the floor of his bedroom, bedsheets tangled around his limbs. His hand flew to his neck. To his mouth.

His lips tingled with pins and needles as though blood had been stemmed from reaching them.

His ankle stung like crazy.

Luca knew he was awake, but part of his mind was still locked into the dream, trying to make sense of the fragments.

His heart thudded against his ribcage. Sweat soaked his body.

He staggered to his feet, grabbed the laptop, rubbed the grogginess from his eyes with the heel of one hand.

The sudden brightness of the screen made his eyes water, but he saw what he was looking for when he opened the browser link.

There, on the hill, on the moor where David slept, was a watchtower.

Just a dream, his logical voice said. *Just a dream made up from everything that's happened. You know it doesn't make sense.*

He looked at his hand, saw the dirt crusted in his palm. Under his nails. The ends of his fingers were pale and wrinkled as though they'd been immersed in water for too long.

The screen suddenly went dark and Luca gasped.

He grabbed the power cable and plugged it in, but nothing happened.

The curtains stirred in a sudden breeze. He walked slowly towards the window, half wondering if he was still dreaming, or if this was a dream within a dream.

The lamp in his father's study was on.

Charles Fox-Waite never worked late for this many nights. Luca checked the time on his phone. 4:52 a.m.

He remembered Lissy's text.

> If you need to talk, you know where I am. Lissy xx

Remembered her single word in his dream. *Stay*.

Luca brought his foot up and rested it on the wicker chair by the window. He pressed his fingers to the blister because it didn't look right. Pain shot up his leg and down into his toes.

He was pressing against raw skin.

The top scar of the blister had been ripped away, exposing a patch of flesh bubbling with pinpricks of fluid.

A high-pitched buzzing began in his ears and Luca had to grab the edge of the windowsill to stop himself tilting sideways.

When the throb began above his right eye he almost screamed. *No. No. This can't be happening now.*

But this was how all his migraines started. And if he didn't listen and close himself off from the light, it would only last longer and involve him puking up his guts for three days.

A sense of unfairness swept over him. He had to get dressed. Ring Lissy. Ring David. So much to do. So much to piece together.

Luca opened his nightstand drawer and popped two strong painkillers from the stash he kept there, praying he'd caught it in time and that it would only last a few hours. He staggered across to his bathroom and cupped his hand under the tap, slipping the pills onto his tongue.

The pain had spread across his temple now, each throb in time with his heartbeat.

He felt the floor move under his feet, clutched the front of the sink to stop himself keeling over.

And as he stumbled back to his bed, flicking the remote to bring down the blackout blinds, as he collapsed onto his pillow and boarded the migraine train into the hell it would deliver him to, a memory crossed his mind.

Of looking down at himself standing naked in the dark overlooking a graveyard. A night breeze swept gently through the trees, making the needle-heavy yew bend to its call.

And the whisper on that breeze as it wound through the ancient stones came from the bones buried deep in the earth, singing the song of the dead and the cursed.

TEXT MESSAGE THREE FROM LUCA – UNOPENED

Hey, hope you're getting some writing done. I've been speaking to Olivia Taverner. Think you said you met her at a conference? Some pretty strange stuff's happened near you. And where your house is? They call it Bone Hollow.
I miss you. Love, Luca xx

WEDNESDAY – DAVID

David decided, as he opened his eyes to a new day, that he hated his own company. Sure, he'd lived alone in London, but that was different. There you could feel the press of people outside of your door, the constant buzz of other lives flitting along around you.

Here it was just mile upon mile of empty, desolate moor. And he felt that emptiness judging him.

He rolled over and pressed his face into the pillow, wondered if staying here all day was an option. That option was swiftly pushed aside. One thing he didn't need was his mind running amok with any extra space he could give it.

He focussed his thoughts on his writing as he swung his legs out of bed and padded to the bathroom.

Dawn had just split the horizon into ripples of colour. Black into smoke, into yellow, into pink, the outline of the hills etched in charcoal. Any other time he would have stopped to admire the spectacle, but this morning he edged along the glass wall, his eyes searching the gloom downstairs.

He picked his way over the floor, went down the stairs, not wanting to glance in the direction of the coffee table.

Jesus, just stop it. Anger flared, heated and sudden. He marched into the living area, fixed his gaze on the table.

His limbs softened.

There was nothing there.

Of course there's nothing there, there's a bloody deadbolt on the door.

A smile touched his lips. He felt lighter, brighter, his whole mood shifting from black to joyous pink just like the colours of the dawn.

Kettle on. Laptop booted. Vitamins swallowed.

There was almost a spring in his step as he munched a slice of toast slathered in butter and wandered over to his desk.

Words flew from his fingertips, syntax galloping around his brain at a rate he knew was sure to give him the bones of something magnificent.

He felt invincible, just like the old days. Page after page of effortless writing, the story alive in his mind. The outside world and everything that had happened to take him here faded into a soft blur.

A scene floated through his head of Imelda, her voice shaky with rare emotion, telling him this would be an automatic bestseller.

His fingers raced over the keypads so quickly that the paragraphs he typed were filled with red underlines, but he didn't care, he didn't have time to go back and correct them, the story demanded he forget and carry on. He bloody loved this feeling, and it had been far too long since it had graced him with its presence.

Over the fucking hill, am I? The thought appeared in his mind and he made a noise in his throat that sounded like triumph.

He'd make those damned critics eat their snooty remarks. He hoped they'd choke on them.

It was only the grumbling of his stomach and the failing light that finally broke the spell.

He glanced down at the word count. Thirteen thousand words. The buzz of achievement raced through his veins. Imelda would be speechless, and that didn't happen often.

As he waited for the frozen chicken burgers to cook, nursing a celebratory glass of whisky, he contemplated life here might not be so bad after all.

He wandered up the stairs to gaze out at the moor. The dark hulk of the watchtower stood on the hill, outlined against the graphite grey sky.

His scalp prickled and he took a step back from the window. It was too dark to see anything, but he felt as if someone was watching him from up there. *Someone, or something.*

After a day where everything had glittered with positivity, the feeling dragged him down so quickly he felt like he was in a lift in freefall.

And then the scent twisted from the shadows, catching him completely off balance. Like smelling newly cut grass in the middle of the night, or rain-soaked earth in the sterile confines of an airport.

It was the scent of old books. Of yellowed paper and faded ink. And something else. A particular scent he associated with a night he had buried in a very deep grave. One he had erected a mausoleum over to stop himself wandering in unawares.

A scent synonymous with Charles Fox-Waite. He tried to push it away but the corpse in this grave wasn't dead and it needed to make him squirm like a worm at the end of a hook.

†

It was Imelda who saw the photo first, and by the time she had hung up on him to wade through damage control, his phone wouldn't stop ringing or interrupting him with notifications. He remembered sitting in the ever-increasing dark of late afternoon, staring into space, numb with disbelief that his whole career had just slid sideways into what could only be described as a colossal dung heap.

His first thought then hadn't been for Luca. It had been for his own skin, and how he was going to salvage anything positive from the shitstorm.

They always say there's no such thing as bad publicity, but this? This upended that particular piece of wisdom and throttled it without mercy.

He was waiting for one particular name to flash up on his screen. The only name he would respond to.

When Charles Fox-Waite appeared, David answered on its second ring.

'Is it true? What the actual fuck, David?'

And then David knew he had crossed a line too far, as Charles rarely swore, called it a lazy use of language.

'I'm sorry.' It was all David had. He waited for the explosion that never came, as the watery sun set below the rooftops opposite.

'Tonight. Seven-thirty. You will end it with him then. And then we will talk.'

Charles didn't wait for David to answer. The line went dead in his hand.

And only then did he think of what this was going to do to Luca.

†

The winter wind stung his skin as he climbed out of the taxi at the end of the fashionable street where the Fox-Waites lived.

The taxi drivers usually recognised him and they would banter back and forth, and he would leave them with a more than generous tip and a story they could tell in the local pub. This time he'd pulled up the collar of his coat and sank into his shoulders, as though this might render him invisible.

David stood at the bottom of the stone steps leading to the large black door. Two carriage lanterns burned at either side. How many times had he run up these steps in the last thirty years? But now he was entering not as an old friend, but as someone who had single-handedly muddied all the glittering waters he had ever sailed upon.

He blew out a breath through his lips and pulled his shoulders back. Time to face the music and hope he could survive the dance.

He let the fox head knocker fall against the door. The sound seemed to echo in the hallway beyond.

The door swung open. Charles met his gaze. David tried to read his face, but Charles had donned his business mask, and even David couldn't read behind that.

He followed Charles down the immaculate, polished hallway, the sound of their shoes breaking the silence.

Only when they were inside the study with the door closed did he launch into his well-rehearsed speech.

'Look, I'm sorry. I know I messed up. I never meant for it to go this far, but you know what Luca is like. Once he gets a hold of something he doesn't let go.' When he was through, David leant against one of the bookshelves, the heel of his hands resting on the gleaming wood surface. He tried what he hoped was an apologetic sigh.

Charles stood by the window. The curtains were open and David could see a light burning in Luca's room in the other wing of the house.

He was blatantly aware he was shifting the blame squarely onto Luca's slim shoulders, using the fact that Charles had never seemed to have any love for his son as a wall to build his own defence upon.

It was a shitty thing to do.

'Do you realise how this makes me look, David? How it affects the status of the company?'

His tone was very composed, but David could sense the anger flickering behind the words.

'Of all the people in the world you could choose, David, you chose Luca. Not your wisest decision.'

'I know.' David half wished Charles would crack and spew angry words in his direction. After all, he'd just found out that his oldest friend had been fucking his son. 'Imelda is trying to pick up the pieces. If anyone can smooth this over, it's her.'

And there he was again, shifting the emphasis onto someone else.

Charles didn't reply, and David found himself studying his old friend's profile against the lamplight. It was a strong profile. The square jaw, the slightly Roman nose, the high brow. They had often joked that Charles was probably some kind of Roman emperor in a past life. David quietly pondered he was probably the kind who put those who displeased him into a blood-soaked arena.

A noise pierced the silence. Feet ran down the stairs. Allegra Fox-Waite's voice followed by another louder one. Luca.

David's gaze swept towards the door. His mouth ran dry.

Charles appeared at his side, his eyes storm-grey. 'You will end it now.'

The subject was not up for discussion.

The door swung open and Luca stood back to let his father leave. No words were exchanged between them. And David wondered if they'd all been said before he arrived.

It felt all wrong. He was going to end this relationship standing in Charles's study. The space wasn't meant for anything intimate. It was a bad place for Luca.

He waited for Luca to say something. They both waited for each other to say something. But it was all in their eyes.

Luca took a step backwards and shook his head. David flinched at the pain in Luca's face, as the dawning realisation hit.

Luca had been praying David would refuse to bow down to pressure, that he wouldn't sacrifice what they had. And now Luca knew his worst fears had come true.

'I'm so sorry, Luca.' David knew he was saying that a lot tonight. And he really was sorry. But whether that was only because he'd been found out was anybody's guess.

Part of him wanted to open his arms, to let Luca run into them, but if he did, he knew his resolve would shatter. It was better this way.

'You can't . . .' The words fell from Luca's lips. 'What about everything you said?' His eyes were wide, slightly shell-shocked, as though he'd been caught in the headlights of a car.

Ah, those words. David bit the inside of his cheek as they rushed over him like ice-cold water.

Hey, I've got you, don't worry. This isn't wrong. *Their first kiss.*

We go as slow as you want, okay? I don't want to lose you, Luca. *The night David took Luca back to his house.*

You're safe with me. You don't have to tell me anything until you're ready. *A few days later, as Luca began to unfurl like a parched rose towards him.*

You make me happy, Luca. Really happy. If you ever leave me for some rock star, let me down easy, okay? *The night on the beach, when everything was warm and golden and nothing could touch them.*

What happens if we get found out? *Luca as they stood looking out over the London skyline from the balcony of a penthouse flat.* We roll with it. *David's glib reply, which didn't really answer anything.*

Luca inched towards him and David steeled himself to say what he knew he had to say. He reached out, wanting to run his fingers down Luca's cheek, then checked himself and snatched his hand back.

A strange thought rushed unbidden into his mind. Sometimes beautiful things were meant to be hidden behind a plate glass window. To be admired from afar, too delicate to be tainted by touch.

'Tell me what I have to do to keep you,' Luca whispered. 'We can meet again, in secret, get a place far away from here, where no one will know us . . .'

His words tumbled out in a yearning torrent of hopeful naivety.

David shook his head, curled his fingers into his palm.

'We can't, Luca. Life doesn't work like that. It was fun while it lasted but we both knew it couldn't go anywhere, right?'

'I thought it was going somewhere.' Luca's whisper, raw with ragged pain.

'You'll find someone else. You'll be happy again.'

David had been on the receiving end of a similar speech a very long time ago. He knew how much it hurt. How much Luca's world was tumbling down around his ears right now.

He wanted to say Luca had been special, was special, that he had meant all the words he had said. But that would be cruel.

Best to cut it all away cleanly, so the wound could heal.

'It's over, Luca. Time for us both to move on.'

If Luca broke down now, David wasn't sure how he'd manage to walk away. He was relying on the fact that Luca had been brought up in this house, where real emotions were hidden behind social etiquette. He was praying that Luca fell back into that snare to give him a chance to escape.

Another shitty thing to do.

As he pushed himself away from the bookcase and strode towards the door, he knew he was leaving Luca in pieces. Hollowed out. Shocked to the core.

Luca had given David his absolute trust, and David had sacrificed it all on the altar of his career.

As David walked out on Luca's life, Charles was waiting outside the study door.

'We'll talk later, David,' was all he said before David found the door firmly closed in his face.

He should have demanded he be part of Luca's dressing-down, to defend him, but David left him there alone to face his father's displeasure.

None of it had been Luca's fault. It was David who had made the first move. David who should have known that eventually it would all be crushed into dust.

But he did it anyway.

†

David had no idea why this awful scene had come back to haunt him in all of its terrible technicolour, but as it slowly skulked back into its grave it took his hunger with it. He made himself pick through the chicken, which by now had cremated itself around the edges.

The prospect of another silent evening loomed, thick and dark and uninviting.

He contemplated writing again but decided he didn't want to jinx his golden efforts from earlier. He contemplated taking a bath, a good long hot soak with a book. He contemplated packing all of his personal belongings and waiting by the door for Imelda, visions of tying a luggage label around his neck like some British wartime refugee child, only this time the child was desperate to return to the city.

He contemplated reading Luca's text messages.

Of all of these ideas, only one won out. Twenty minutes later he eased himself into a bath hot enough to melt the skin from his flesh.

Bubbles encased his body and he let himself relax into the heat as he opened his book. After a few minutes, his eyelids grew heavy.

A sharp noise clattered into the silence. He sat up, felt the immediate chill against his skin.

It came again, this time lasting longer than the first. The sound of something collapsing onto a hard floor.

Downstairs.

Panic shot up his throat, lodging there like a cold lump of clay. *Had he deadbolted the door?*

His reason answered that he hadn't. But that's only because he hadn't been outside since yesterday and the door had been bolted all this time.

Wrapped up in a towel, he padded across the bedroom and along the walkway, leaving damp footprints in his wake.

In the gloom of the lower level all was quiet. All was still.

He paused halfway down the stairs, his heart rate galloping into overdrive, his limbs tingling with adrenaline.

And then the sound again, this time softer, something crumbling.

David flicked on the light and the kitchen emerged from the darkness.

It was very evident from first glance what was causing the noise. The rain of plaster dust on the floor tiles said it all. But that wasn't where he found his gaze lingering.

On the wall a large crack spider-webbed from a hole. A hole with something sprouting from it. An impossible thing sprouting from it.

The jagged end of a spike of blackthorn had birthed from the plaster.

He walked over, raised his hand to touch . . . and his fingertips came away wet.

Plants could grow through walls, but not this quickly. Not in a new house.

He took a step back, until he could feel the press of the kitchen island against his spine.

And David Lansdown felt the shrill scream of something inevitable against his bones.

Something outside was determined to come in.

Thursday – Luca

Luca drifted in and out of his migraine purgatory. Distant voices seemed to tune in and out and then fade into static.

He wanted to sleep but knew that sleep held no rest.

She was there. Mary of the Moor. The Bone Crone. A hunched shape on the edge of his dreamscape. A blight he always knew existed. When she spoke, her words sounded like old bones rattling together, speaking a language only she understood.

The lash of rain pelted his window, and in his mind's eye the drumming of the rain became a meandering stream under the summer sun, then an angry river swollen by snow-melt.

But underneath it all Luca felt there was something he had to do.

He forced his eyelids open and was rewarded by an ice-pick jab through his skull. Bright spots floated in his vision and his logic screamed, *Too soon!*

And then a scent rolled out of the dark. A scent he would know anywhere. Leather and bergamot oil and cinnamon. His father's cologne.

Luca's brow creased, then he winced as another sharp pain speared his brain.

What had his father been doing here? He never came to Luca's room.

Very slowly, he rolled onto his side. Someone had left a bottle of water on his nightstand and a bowl on the floor. He was grateful he hadn't ejected the contents of his stomach into the latter.

A stray lock of hair fell across his eyes. He pushed it aside and felt a few strands loosen in his fingers.

He couldn't fathom why. His eyelids closed again. Everything was too heavy. Too painful.

Yet that low thrum of *something* refused to let go.

How long had he been out for?

His fingertips skimmed his phone. He opened his eyes for a split second.

Thursday. It said Thursday. He'd lost a whole day.

He shut one eye. Narrowed his other to a slit. And sent the text sitting in his drafts.

Luca lay his head back against his pillow, his skull feeling as if it was split open, at the mercy of something that had no understanding of haste or need.

**TEXT MESSAGE FOUR FROM LUCA
– UNOPENED**

David, please listen to me.
I've spent a long time looking
at more details and I think what
I've found out is way more than
coincidence. I'm getting really
bad vibes from all of this.
Luca xx

THURSDAY – DAVID

Early morning sunlight arrowed across his bed. David rubbed his gritty eyes and blearily checked the time on his phone. He'd slept with it under his pillow.

The battery was almost dead.

He forced himself to shower and put on clean clothes before heading downstairs, determined to put aside the weird happenings. His steps felt lighter. It was true, sunlight made everything better.

But the smile on his face froze as his gaze fell on the coffee table.

On its polished wooden surface lay another bone.

He ran to the door. The bolts were still fastened.

A sound like a whimper left his throat.

He slid the bolts free and unlocked the door, but his hands were trembling so much it took more than one attempt.

Even the gravel stinging his bare soles didn't stop him from running from the house. He reached the gate, flung it open, curled his hands around the solidity of the wood. His breath hitched in his lungs.

Someone—*something*—had been in his house.

The ice-water dread of it fell upon him like a starving beast, its claws rending away all sense of logic and reality.

But in the mist-laced glow of the dawn as the winter sun rose over the distant hills, the house didn't look threatening at all.

David licked his lips and swallowed. He retreated a few more steps. His feet met a slight dip in the earth and he stumbled, righting himself before he fell.

Outside the gate and the newly built drystone wall that marked his boundary was a depression in the ground, about five feet long. The moor hadn't claimed it as its own, for the soil was bare. David knelt and ran a handful of earth through his fingers.

He took a deep breath. The air here was sharp and unapologetic, filled with feral wildness, much like the landscape.

Slowly, he walked back over the gravel towards the open door. He would ring Imelda, ask her to send someone out to check the house. But even as he made this decision he knew it wouldn't explain the bone.

No, he'd just have to hold on for a few more days. Imelda said she'd be across on Saturday. He could do this. She had said something as they sat overlooking the Thames. Something he had only rolled his eyes in reply to.

It's perfect for you, David. What horror writer doesn't want to live in a possessed house?

But that was just throwaway talk, surely?

What if the people who built this house had unearthed something unspeakable? What if Luca had been right all along about the presence of other things?

David desperately needed to hear Luca's voice.

He remembered the fading battery as he walked back into the house.

Forty-five minutes later the contents of just about every drawer lay strewn around the floor. Sweat pooled under his arms and in the small of his back.

The phone charger was nowhere to be found.

The air was still. The light weakened. His gaze flicked to the window wall. Grey clouds huddled in clumps, rapidly covering the watery sun.

He was suddenly hyper aware of sand running through an hour glass

With a cry of anguish he hurtled towards the stairs, climbing them two at a time, careering across the walkway towards the bedroom. He flung himself on the bed, scrabbled for the reassuring comfort of the phone still under his pillow.

The battery level had gone from orange to red.

Just as David pressed the screen to finally read Luca's words, the battery died.

'No.' He shook the phone. Turned it off then on again in a fit of desperate hopefulness. 'No, no, no!' The wail fell from his lips.

Now he was truly alone.

He sat on the edge of the bed and rocked to and fro, his hands wrapped around his body, clutching his elbows.

The sound of the letterbox clattered into his seclusion. Such a normal sound.

He roused himself and padded downstairs, could see the folded piece of white paper laying on the mat.

It had been torn from the same pad as the cryptic note on his day of arrival.

He scooped it from the mat, read the spidery scrawl.

Mr. Lansdown. Why are you still here? The land doesn't want you. Haven't you had enough warnings?

David yanked open the door.

An animal skull sat by his threshold. Shreds of pink flesh clung to its empty sockets.

The wind brought the sound of a small dog yapping.

†

A little while later he forced himself to eat a slice of toast, but it tasted like cardboard.

The sun had forced itself through the low bank of sullen cloud cover, bathing the house in a soft, diffused light. This place had two faces. And even with all the words at his fingertips David knew he'd never be able to explain how it made him feel. How alive with shadows it became when the sun went down.

He needed to get out. Clear his head. Imelda wanted him focussed, but when he wasn't concentrating on his story he had begun to pick himself apart, layer by layer, exposing everything he had worked so hard to bury.

Deals he had made. People he'd trodden on.

Like the woman who asked him to sign one of his books for charity who he'd never gotten back to. Lovers he'd left when another pretty face came along.

But none of them lived in his head like Luca.

He contemplated whether Luca might have been *the one* and raged at himself for destroying that chance to save his career.

And for what? He didn't need any more money. Had a catalogue of books he was proud of. He could cash it all in. Beg for Luca's forgiveness. Get a dog to keep him company. Write under a pen name. Self-publish.

Gather Luca to him. Never let him go.

For a moment the sheer deliciousness of these thoughts overwhelmed him.

He grabbed his jacket, thrust his feet into his boots, and stormed from the house. The door slammed behind him and he winced as the sound rolled across the heather.

He bypassed the gate, climbed over the wall, his gaze trained upon the ancient pathway that led past his house. The Corpse Road, where countless feet had journeyed with their dead. Journeyed towards the nearest church through rain and snow and burning heat.

For some this must have lasted days, and David shivered as he thought about travelling with the slowly rotting corpse of someone you loved wrapped only in a basic shroud. Coffins were for the rich.

He made a mental note to try to use this in his story, but as he turned left, for no other reason than his feet led him that way, he wondered if he was kidding himself. What he was writing was a narrative about a man forced into a life of loneliness, whose misdeeds came back to haunt him in the night. It was no Ebenezer Scrooge or Jacob Marley tale, but he was writing it so the reader would wonder if what his protagonist suffered was true or a figment of his disillusioned mind.

The freezing air hurt his lungs, made his eyes and nose stream, but there was a cleansing feel about it. The track dipped to the left then carried onwards past a pile of stones that might once have been a house. David edged through a small gap between a drystone wall and a ruined gate beached into the thick mud. The occasional sheep in the field beyond raised its head, jaw chewing. A group of dark birds circled above him.

At the top of the next rise he rested, the landscape spilling out before him, the colours a blending roll of wheat and moss and copper, ending in the pewter-coated, flat-backed mountains hunched under the winter sky.

From here he could see the silver back of the river below glinting in the sun.

And something else. *Someone* else.

The woman he had seen on his visit to the watchtower, the one he was almost sure left the note.

Fury sandblasted through his veins. He set off towards her, determined this time to make her speak to him.

She was sitting on a large rock by the water's edge, the shooting stick resting on her lap, the dog snuffling in the grass at her feet.

As he marched across he could see a pile of white stones on the top of the rock next to her.

As he strode ever closer, he saw that they were bones.

'Are you the one who's been leaving the notes?' He tried to keep his voice level, but anger trembled on their edges.

'Louisa Hardcastle,' she said, planting the tip of her shooting stick into the grass as she stood. 'And that's Fetch. Not that he ever brings anything back.'

'David,' he offered, omitting any mention of a surname. But that didn't seem to bother her.

'I know who you are,' she said. There was a pause as Fetch found a rabbit hole, and they both watched him dig furiously. 'You shouldn't be here.'

'I'm working on a new book,' he replied, wondering why he felt the need to explain.

'That might be, but she doesn't want you here. None of us do. Not after what happened to Bone Hollow.'

'I'm sorry?' The name didn't mean anything to David, but the fact he wasn't welcome wasn't a surprise. Although he didn't know who 'she' was.

'Bone Hollow. It's where that monstrosity is. Where you're staying. There's reasons why no one built there.'

'So it was you?' He brought the conversation back around. His eyes strayed to the pile of bones. 'Did you leave the bones in the house?'

She rested both hands on the shooting stick, fixed him with an appraising stare that made him look away.

'Yes and no. I left the notes, but I've never been in that house. Maybe someone is looking out for you.'

'Someone has a key to my house?' Despite the chill, David could feel his cheeks flushing.

'I don't know, Mr. Lansdown. If they have they are doing you a favour. She collects bones, you see, always has. If she finds some where you are, maybe she'll leave you alone. Or maybe she's leaving them for you, to let you know she's there. These are for her.'

Louisa glanced down to the pile of vertebrae bones stacked in a tower. 'To try to persuade her to rest. Mary of the Moor, David. The Bone Crone. Look her up before she does the same to you.'

Her gaze fell to the tumbling current of the river. She muttered something under her breath.

'If I were you, Mr. Lansdown, I'd leave right now. While you still can.'

She nodded and set off along the river bank, Fetch loping ahead, leaving David dumbstruck, the anger turning to disquietude in his gut.

He marched off up the hill, Louisa's words spinning in his head like a juggler's plates on a stick. He needed to keep them all spinning until he could make sense of what she'd said, but already he could sense some slowing, wobbling, about to crash to the floor.

Superstition. The word hissed in his head, coiling itself against his thoughts.

And yet, Louisa had seemed perfectly calm. Perfectly sane.

Was she just trying to scare him away?

He raged against the fact he couldn't do his own research. Until Imelda arrived with his usual phone, he was trapped in his own quagmire of uncertainty.

The house appeared as he crested the hill and he tried to imagine how the landscape would have looked without it.

And he had to admit, even with its sympathetic stonework it didn't look like it belonged.

Reluctantly, he trudged back down towards it, his hands stuffed into his coat pockets, his nose streaming.

The flash of red caught his eye from a distance. His mouth twisted. It was on the gate, which swung back and forth in the brisk wind. On the air came the teeth-clenching sound of the hinges squealing.

No, it couldn't be . . .

He slowed, his heart rate spiking, disgust curling his lip.

But it was.

On the gate to the house that stood on Bone Hollow, someone had left him a gift.

A gleaming mass of pink entrails wound around the top of the first bar, one purpled kidney swinging obscenely in the breeze.

Thursday – David

David Lansdown sat on his bed, numb from the inside out. He was having trouble processing whether the entrails were a warning, or just some fucked-up local atonement.

These are for her, to try to persuade her to rest, Louisa had said.

Nothing more than country poppycock, he told himself. *What else do they have to do but live in the past?*

Shivers wracked his body. He wasn't sure if he was coming down with something or just plain terrified and unwilling to accept it. He pulled on a thick sweater and, with his hand trailing along the metal rail on the walkway, began a slow descent downstairs.

The blackthorn spike in the kitchen wall had pushed itself through by a few more inches. His brain dredged up a morsel from a previous book. *A 'black rod' is a blackthorn wand of sharp thorns. A Witch's wand.*

He shrugged on a jacket and went outside, averting his eyes from the gate. There was no need to calculate which bush the spike had come from because there were no bushes, just a wall of stone.

Which only left one option. One impossible option.

The blackthorn was under the earth.

He knew, instinctively, that it had grown here before the house. Had been torn out. Yet here it was, crawling through the fucking walls, refusing to die.

†

By the time he pulled himself together, most of the light had leeched from the sky.

He found himself staring out of the window wall again, some compulsion making his eyes search the rolling terrain.

A group of birds, black specks in the distance, whirled and dove against the drab grey blanket of sky.

He watched them for a while, envious of their freedom, of their unnecessary baggage. They became the sole focus of his attention as they danced across the sky, coming closer by the minute.

Now he could see they were crows. He counted nine. Could almost see the feathers on their wingtips as they cavorted together in some wild frenzy. He could hear their cries and some part of him thrilled to the sound.

Were they the ones that had circled above him earlier?

Just as he was about to tear himself away, they stopped their aerial dance. Each one seemed to hover in the air like a bird of prey sighting a mouse.

David took a step back, but he was held in their thrall.

A single bird moved away from the group.

And then it dove towards the window wall, its wings flat against its body.

His back met the rail and a sudden pain shot up his spine.

It has to stop, he thought. *It has to stop.*

But the crow was so close now he could see the glint from its eyes as it hurtled towards him.

There was a sickening crunch as its body met the glass. It dropped like a stone, fine feathers drifting on the air.

Another bird split from the group.

David could only watch in absolute horror as it repeated the action of the first. This time the impact left a bloody slime against the window.

One by one, the others hurtled towards the same fate, quicker now, so that David's whole being was filled with the awful sound of crushed bones, his sight blighted by smears of blood and ripped feathers, his logic torn into shreds of traumatised revulsion.

It was very quiet in the aftermath of the avian suicide.

Through the gore-streaked glass, it began to rain.

THURSDAY NIGHT – DAVID

The afternoon slid into night.

David Lansdown, esteemed horror author, was coming apart at the seams, thread by horrifying thread.

He downed endless cups of coffee until the caffeine onslaught made his already shaking hands worse.

He ate a bar of chocolate stashed in the fridge, then promptly threw up a brown sludge into the sink.

Sweat coated his skin but he couldn't get warm. He clutched the dead phone to his chest as if it was a wounded creature he was trying to bring back to life. He wished he'd read the texts from Luca.

Every lamp and every light in the house was lit, but still the shadows lurked in each corner.

David turned on his laptop and began to write because it was the only thing he could do. And as he wrote, the chaos of his life seemed to fade slightly until it was just a soft shadow against his edges. He hung onto that feeling like a drowning man.

As the moon rose over the watchtower, he typed the final lines.

> They say the veil thins between the worlds of the living and the dead on All Hallows Eve, but darkness runs rampant on the longest night where it is both king and executioner.
>
> It is on Midwinter's night where those who slumber under the earth open the soil-caked sockets of their eyes. They feel it in the air above, seeping down through earth and grass, this beckoning from the shadows.
>
> Come and play, come and play.
>
> It is a countrywide phenomenon but it is felt more in the wild, open spaces, where the land remembers what has gone before. And none more so than on a certain tract of moorland, home to all manner of supernatural things, a place where history has carved the land into segments but where, if you know where to look, you can

still find burial chambers from the Stone Age and twisted trees with mournful branches who still feel the weight of the noose and its meal.

Villages dot the moorland, the low houses huddled together for comfort, their walls turned to the cruel teeth of the rolling waves of heather and gorse. Those who have dwelt in the village for generations understand that the moor asks for what it wants. They understand that on Midwinter's Eve they must stay in front of their firesides, not be drawn to the shadows that pass their windows with the curtains pulled tight.

For the dead will walk, gathering any in their path, because this night is theirs and the track they walk upon is an ancient stretch of land they have travelled before.

All hail the Corpse Road. Pity the living who stumble blindly into its maw.

He set the printer to churn out the pages.

Suddenly he was very glad he had put all his affairs in order before he left London.

He grabbed a pencil and scrawled on the title page as it emerged from the printer—*For Luca, the bringer of light.*

It was what his name meant.

He climbed the stairs, avoiding the wet patches on the treads and along the walkway. It was pointless mopping them up.

A coughing fit wracked his body and he stopped halfway to the bedroom. He wasn't surprised the same musty smell was there, stronger this time. It was the water. The fucking water that wouldn't go away.

When he walked into the bedroom, the lamp in the corner softly glowing, black mould spider-webbed its way across the walls. Capillary-like. Relentless.

The sheets on the bed were slightly wet.

He understood why the people who built this house left so quickly, why Imelda had been able to snap it up, fully furnished, for a song.

The moor didn't want it here. Its presence was a blight, an insult to something that had gone before.

In a flash of understanding David realised why Luca had sent so many texts. They were warnings.

Dear God, Luca, I failed you in so many ways.

In the still of the night there came a scratching against the glass of the window wall.

David tore a lamp from the nightstand, yanked off the shade, and coiled the cable around it. He wrapped his fingers around its length. Even though he knew it would be useless in defending himself against whatever was out there.

A slow scraping rolled from the darkened lower level.

He forced himself from the threshold of the bedroom.

An almighty crashing noise came as something heavy fell to the floor. It echoed around the vaulted ceiling.

He looked down into the blackness.

The coffee table top lay adrift from its base.

On the stone which had upheld it, a huddled shape crouched.

He charged to the top of the staircase, a roar which held both pure terror and desperate bravado spilling from his throat.

In that moment he was ready to face whatever force was out there.

As soon as his feet hit the water, David Lansdown knew it was all over. His legs went from underneath him, his spine crashing against the wall. He tried to grab for the staircase rail but it slipped through his fingers. And then he was tumbling, tumbling down the stairs, head over heels, each tread delivering a fresh bout of pain.

The back of his head met the polished wooden floor of the lower level. He felt his brain rock inside his skull. And then there was nothing but a tunnel of darkness and the taste of his own blood on his tongue.

Thursday – Luca

Luca awoke in the dead of night. At least, he thought it was night. His head still throbbed and his body felt like he'd been bounced off a wall, but the worst of the pain had gone. His stomach grumbled.

He gingerly eased himself off the bed and padded to the bathroom. As he washed his hands he could see the reflection of his phone in the mirror.

A light flashed in one corner.

His heart lurched but he made himself walk slowly across. And then it fell.

Luca narrowed his eyes to try to shield the screen glare. A text from Lissy saying she was staying in Paris, as another client she'd gone to see had food poisoning and they'd had to move the meeting. She signed off with,

> Ring me anytime, okay?
> Remember, we share the Stupid xx

A smile touched his lips. The Stupid was in reference to one of his many past predicaments. He'd told her back then what was bothering him was stupid, and so the Stupid was born, a message between them that said nothing was too minor to talk about.

He let his eyes run over her words again. Neither Lissy nor Luca ever used text talk. Never abbreviated anything. Lissy had once said that it was obvious they both must have been around in the eighteenth century, penning letters written in midnight ink, sealed with their family crest.

But they both knew it was because they were brought up in a house where words were something never to be trifled with.

Luca's stomach churned. He dragged his mind back to the present. He needed to go and find something bland to eat to keep the migraine from reappearing, even though he knew he really shouldn't be moving around too much.

A single lamp burned on the console table by the entrance hall door, casting shadows across the wall. Luca crept downstairs, his bare feet silent on the tiled floor as he made his way to the kitchen.

He grabbed a banana from the fruit bowl, unzipped it and carefully ate it in small bites.

It was only as he made his way back along the hallway that he heard his father's voice. Luca stopped dead in his tracks, his ear cocked towards the sound.

It was coming from the study.

He backtracked and turned the corner into the separate hallway that led there. A thin, flickering light shone from under the study door.

His father's voice came again. Then silence.

Maybe he was talking on the phone to someone in another time zone? But it didn't sound like his father's phone voice, which was self-assured and pointed, the kind of voice people listened to and didn't interrupt.

It was softer, more open to whatever the other person was saying.

Luca knew he should just go back upstairs but something made him stand there, as though he were a small boy again waiting for his father's attention.

He put his ear against the door, felt the polished wood smooth against his cheek. But the door was thick and he couldn't make out any words.

Luca stole along the corridor to the door at the far end. It was the side entrance into the garden pavilion, recently constructed as just another space where his mother could showcase her beautiful and expensive trinkets. It had bi-fold doors to the east, a retracting glass door to the south, and an all-glass bay to the west.

Luca thought it was like a goldfish bowl. But that thought was now far from his mind as he unlatched the door and crept from the pavilion along the small paved pathway that led to the side of his father's study.

The sash window stood open a few inches.

With his heart lodged in his throat, Luca eased himself closer. Cold leeched into the soles of his feet and already his exposed skin felt half-frozen.

He pressed his back against the creeping greenery that trailed all along the walls and peered around the edge of the window frame. The flickering light came from a candle set in the middle of his father's desk.

But that wasn't what forced an audible gasp from Luca's throat. It was the fact the candle stood next to the open Ouija board.

Luca's thoughts became a jumble of confused chaos. He gulped in mouthfuls of freezing air as his head began to spin.

He could hear his father muttering under his breath. Could hear the roll of the planchette as it slid across the board.

'Ah,' his father's voice crept from the window. 'So you ask at last.'

It wasn't the words that made Luca's stomach threaten to purge what he'd just eaten, it was the almost satisfied tone of his father's voice.

A fetid smell drifted from the slightly open window. Burnt hair. Luca's nose wrinkled in disgust.

The planchette moved again. His father laughed.

'I don't think it will be too long. And the sweetest thing about all of this is that he really has no idea what is coming.'

Luca's eyes widened. He bit the inside of his lip, felt the warm copper tang flood onto his tongue.

He.

Who was *he*?

How long had his father been using the Ouija board? Is this how he had gone from strength to strength over the years, his star ever rising? Making deals with the things he publicly scoffed about?

Luca shivered, and then the most horrible feeling gripped him by the throat.

What if the person his father was talking about was David?

†

Luca crept back to his room.

None of it made sense. But the more he thought about the person being David, the more the ball of dread in his gut grew.

Charles Fox-Waite had never let anyone make him look a fool. But David had. There'd been heated discussions on the phone and no doubt in person. Luca wasn't sure how much resentment his father still harboured.

David's last two books hadn't been as well received as the others. The media spouted he was losing his touch, ever ready to drag their former darling off his pedestal and sing the praises of someone new.

And now David was alone in a house on a moor with no means of escape. A place Luca already knew came with its own unearthly history.

If something happened to him out there, there would be no ties back to his father. Charles Fox-Waite never left any loose ends to hang himself with.

Luca sat on his bed, images of David flashing through his head.

The après-migraine hangover throbbed in the back of his skull.

His phone vibrated with an email. Olivia.

His eyes scanned her succinct style he was beginning to recognise. The words settled against his heart like an iced fist.

I feel it's important that you know the following facts, Luca.

From one of my sources – a children's rhyme:

Mary, Mary, cast a bone.
Buried deep, beneath the stone.
If it moved her flesh will moan
Mary, Mary, cursed crone.

And from the diary of William de Morcote – Parson of the Church of St. Lawrence (and I've translated this).

Mary of the Moor laid to rest at Bone Hollow, as none would have her close for fear she would walk from her grave. 'For revenge did blacken her ungodly heart.'

Instinct tells me there's a very definite chance that Mary of the Moor is the Mary in the children's rhyme. The wandering figure reported by so many people over the years.

If you'd like to discuss further, you can ring me at the number below.

Luca knew he didn't have the luxury of time. Knew he couldn't explain himself by text. He picked up his phone and rang David's number. It went straight to an automated voicemail.

Something was wrong. Luca felt it like a cold whisper against his ear.

His sudden migraine. The mark on his foot that had bled with no reason. The feeling that reality had twisted in on itself.

He only had one choice. Not that it was a sensible one. And if it ended with David slamming the door in his face at least he'd know David was okay. Screw sitting back and just waiting.

He dressed quickly, swallowed a couple more painkillers, and threw a few things into a holdall. His car keys had been confiscated by his father, no doubt to stop him from visiting David, but Luca wasn't going to let that stop him.

Luca pulled on a thick jacket and slipped into his sister's room. He knew where she kept her own set of keys.

What he was doing would more than likely seal the lid of his coffin as his father's son. But the ever-building dread pulsing through his veins drowned out any fear for his own future.

He fired off one more short, frantic text to David, even though he knew it wouldn't be read. With Lissy's car keys in his hand he stole out of the back door and across the darkened lawn, casting a single glance backwards towards the study.

It lay in complete darkness as though nothing untoward had ever happened. As though this grand Georgian mansion had never opened itself to what lay beyond the veil. And as Luca opened the door to Lissy's car, he was met with the overwhelming feeling that he had never known his father at all.

TEXT MESSAGE FIVE FROM LUCA – UNOPENED

GET OUT, GET OUT, GET OUT!

Thursday – Charles Fox-Waite

Charles Fox-Waite retired to his bedroom after tidying away the contents in his study. He placed his watch in the velvet box in the drawer of his nightstand, by the coiled cable of the phone charger one of the removal men had made sure found its way into his possession. He brushed a few strands of Luca's hair from his arm.

He could still smell the acrid burn as he held it to the candle flame. His final agreement in the bargain he had made so long ago.

It had worked well, getting Lissy's meeting changed. She would stay over, no doubt running up a handsome restaurant tab, but he didn't regret that. He was proud of the woman his daughter had become and wished yet again that Luca had some of her characteristics.

He was old enough to remember when women only had menial jobs in publishing, but Lissy had carved out a promising career for herself through sheer hard work and determination. The future of his company would be safe in her hands.

But he didn't need her here, putting ideas in Luca's head.

He had to keep Luca in the house for things to work out as he'd planned.

Luca. He took a long swallow of the brandy he had brought upstairs, felt the burn slip down his throat as he tried to stem the surge of frustration. Sometimes he wondered if Luca was actually his. They had absolutely nothing in common, and try as he might he couldn't dredge up any feelings of affection for the boy.

Although now that the plans were made, it shouldn't have come as much surprise.

He hadn't really felt any tenderness with regard to Luca's feelings when news of the affair hit the fan, more concerned about how the scandal would affect David's new release and the company profits.

But, of course, he had to act like he had Luca's best interest at heart. And Charles Fox-Waite was very good at acting.

Telling Luca he had spoken to David was an outright lie. As was the idea that David didn't want to come back.

Necessary lies were only hopeful truths.

Charles thought about that long-ago night in the tunnel more frequently than he liked to admit. Part of him was always waiting for whatever had been there to come back and claim what he'd bargained away.

He'd tried to overrule its hold on his thoughts by publicly denouncing anything supernatural unless it was within the pages of his writers, fuelling his lifestyle.

But on that New Year's Eve night he knew it hadn't forgotten.

It left a permanent reminder. The start of a new year but with an old debt to pay.

When Luca's affair with David hit the headlines, Charles kept all of the intense fury and indignation hidden. It simmered slowly, roiling away, becoming a poison he knew he had to purge.

And that was when he found the Ouija board on the Dark Web. Well, not him personally, of course. He had many minions for tasks like this. Tasks he found distasteful. He would never soil his own hands digging up the dirt on other publishing houses or their authors.

Minions. Paid enough to keep their mouths firmly closed.

The source said it was 'live', which was a very ironic choice of word for something that summoned the dead.

But it had proved itself already, and tonight was its crowning glory.

Charles had no idea in previous conversations what had breached the thin, blurred line separating the living and the dead. He imagined it as some kind of vast supernatural playground, the damned drifting in and out of the board's call.

But he knew as soon as the right voice answered him. It made the skin across his scalp tighten, churned the contents of his gut into a liquid sludge.

A terrible but exhilarating thought slid from the confines of his mind, one that had been festering like an inflamed abscess. He both hated himself for even thinking it and admired the sheer brilliance of the strategy.

There was a way to pay his old debt—dissolve the weight which had clung to him all of his life—and to rid himself of a problem which wasn't going to get any better.

Give me something precious, it had demanded.

Tonight he delivered on his promise from so long ago.

And really, there was nothing more precious than a first-born son.

THURSDAY – LUCA

Headlights sliced through the thick darkness, appearing and disappearing as the car sped along the winding country road. The engine growled under the onslaught of the driver's agitation, the sound ripping the silence into tattered shreds.

A fine drizzle fell from the sombre sky, falling through air damp and twisted by winter's hand. The car was travelling too fast for the weather conditions.

But the driver didn't care. He had lost all semblance of self-preservation on his long journey here.

All that mattered was getting to David, so he could warn him of the danger he was in.

Luca didn't even know if David would let him in the house. After all, he hadn't answered any of his texts. But Luca had to try. He'd never forgive himself if something awful happened, and he could feel that something awful crawling under his skin, urging him to *hurry, hurry.*

Hours on the road had reduced his whole existence to the ribbon of darkness unfolding before him and the twin beams of light knifing through it.

Lissy's car wasn't quite as powerful as his own. He was pushing his luck as he forced it to its limitations. Around a sharp S-bend, the back end slid, and for a moment he let it go, his gloved hands loosening on the steering wheel. A high bank of hawthorn scraped along the side of the car, the screech firing his senses into autopilot. He corrected the slide, and the tyres scrabbled for grip, and it was just human against machine with the cold moon hanging in the branches of the winter-bare trees.

He imagined what his father would say if he got the call that his son had ploughed himself into a ditch.

A grimace tightened on his lips as the car straightened, loose gravel from the edge of the road peppering the underside.

Charles Fox-Waite's first consideration would be that his son had flagrantly disobeyed what he had told him. He would check his son's car keys were still locked in the safe. And then he would march outside to the garage and discover Luca had taken Lissy's car to drive to the place he had been expressly forbidden to go.

Luca didn't want to dwell on the fallout. It might involve a stay in one of those exclusive rehabs, the kind never mentioned in polite society. It was possible ending up dead in a ditch might be the best option.

His mother would try to calm Charles by placing her hand on his arm. The diamonds on her rings would catch the light from the fire. Such a cold light, Luca had always thought, as he had stood before them both, waiting to be verbally torn apart yet again.

Luca's mind was filled with remembrance and the inevitable repercussions as the car sped out of the sharp bend. The headlights flared, opening up a wide tunnel of light. A shape shuffled along the edge of the road, hunched up against the driving drizzle and the cold.

One sharp inhalation of breath as Luca's mind registered the shape as a person. He braked hard, his seatbelt locking as the tyres screamed.

Those slow, freeze-frame seconds before something terrible happened snared Luca in their jaws. He tried to steer around the shape, but one side of the car had slid into the half-frozen ruts a tractor had left, and it wasn't going anywhere but straight ahead.

Luca was barely aware of the hedge disappearing, of the silhouette of trees taking its place. A bone-shaking jar as the car swerved back onto the road, completely out of control. It sped faster as the road dipped, sliding sideways now as the tyres met a patch of black ice.

Everything was noise and chaos and panic.

In the crazed light of the twin beams Luca saw a gate looming ever nearer. Canopies of winter trees lay beyond, and then dark, dark.

So much dark.

As metal met wood and the impact sent splinters of timber skyward, the airbag exploded. Luca felt an excruciating pain as his nose shattered.

And then there was a moment of surreal quiet as the noise of undergrowth scraping and churning under the car stopped.

The car was in flight, the ground beyond the gate a steep drop on a hillside dotted by spruce and pine.

It landed. Luca screamed but his mouth was full of blood.

Bouncing from tree trunk to tree trunk, the car continued on its manic descent. Despite being held to his seat by his belt and the deflating airbag, Luca felt a rib snap.

The windscreen exploded as a wayward branch speared through it. A rush of freezing air. The scent of pine.

Something glinted like a silver ribbon ahead.

The car hit what was left of an old fisherman's shack, the walls collapsed in on each other. It became the perfect and most horrifying platform to launch the car skywards again. This time it flipped, landing with an almighty crash twenty feet farther along.

It careered towards the silver ribbon on its roof, windfall branches punching their way into the cab.

Luca somehow had the presence of mind to jam his elbow against the automatic window button.

The car hit a fallen tree trunk and jerked back onto its wheels before plunging into the rain-swollen river. Freezing water flooded in through the smashed windscreen and driver side window. Trapped between the seat and the floating airbag, Luca struggled to reach the belt buckle. Waves of sharp pain coursed through his side. Blood clogged his throat.

The current toyed with the car, spinning it sideways, deepening his sense of lost reality. For a few seconds, he wondered if simply giving in to the inevitable would be such a bad thing.

But then the reason he was here clawed through his thoughts.

David.

His fingers found the buckle. He pressed. Nothing happened.

Panic took him.

The water was up to his chest now. He could feel the pressure of it, making his snapped rib howl in protest.

Luca closed his eyes, relaxed into the seat, let his limbs go slack. He found the buckle again and instead of jamming his fingers against it, he simply depressed it with one thumb as if this was just an ordinary day in an ordinary life.

The belt came free. He pulled it over his chest, shrugged his shoulder out, ignoring the sharp stabs of pain.

Up to his neck in raging, angry water, Luca grabbed the roof and heaved himself out of his seat. This time the river helped, sweeping him out of what would have been a death trap.

The car spun away from him.

He could see the surface of the water boiling up ahead.

Not too far. I can do this.

He kicked out, each movement of his arms sending excruciating pain through his chest. He gritted his teeth and rode the pain upwards, until finally his head broke the surface and he was gasping, shivering, half-hysterical.

But alive.

He struggled to the bank, hauled himself out, crawled on his elbows and stomach inch by inch until the water only touched his toes.

Luca lay there for a few minutes, trying to come to terms with how he'd cheated death by the skin of his teeth. But he knew he had to move before hyperthermia set in.

He spat out a wad of thick blood and touched his nose. His sinuses screamed.

Very slowly, he tried to draw his legs beneath him but they felt as wobbly as a new-born foal's.

He glanced over his shoulder. There was nothing to suggest a car had ever been here.

Move, Luca.

The voice in his head wasn't coaxing. It was demanding. Almost fevered.

A frown creased his brow.

His flesh started to creep.

His eyes widened.

Something cold and miry wound itself around his ankle.

He wheeled, saw the flesh-shrunken hand with its fingers covering his blister, and understanding pierced Luca's chest like an arrow.

He was marked.

He'd always been marked.

Luca saw the face of the Bone Crone underneath the water, her hair writhing in the current.

And as he was dragged back into the icy depths, a scream tearing from his lungs, the only mercy was that he didn't know his father had sold him to the dead before Luca was even born.

Thursday, 11.59pm – David

David's eyelids flickered. Vomit rose in his throat and he turned his head, ejecting a pool of foul-smelling, bilious sludge.

The house was still in darkness. A sound came from somewhere but he couldn't pinpoint where or what it was.

And then he remembered.

Panic jolted his muscles into action. He rolled over onto his elbow, ignoring the sharp streak of agony which shot up to his shoulder.

Dagger-like points tore at his skin. He winced and turned, saw the snaking mass of the blackthorn covering the floor, a writhing coil of tangles and deadly thorns leading from the hole in the wall, stopping at . . .

He slowly lifted his gaze to find the shape he had seen earlier. It was waiting for him. It was the same one he had seen watching him from the Corpse Road.

He caught the overwhelming scent of damp and decay, saw a skeletal hand emerge from rotted cloth. Before his horrified eyes, the blackthorn crawled around it.

The sound that fell into the dark turned his blood to an icy slush. It was a keening. A wailing. A cry of loss and fury and abject grief.

And David understood then, in a blinding flash of realisation. The depression in the ground outside his gate was made by the stone that now sat in this cursed house.

The coffin stone where countless bodies rested on their way to their cold and lonely graves.

The thing raised its hand and pointed towards David. Or at least, he thought that at first, until he spun around and saw what was waiting for him through the window wall at the other side of the glass.

†

And now he waits in the bed with damp sheets clinging to his skin, sickened to the core. This is all his fault.

Waits in the bedroom with the mould oozing across the ceiling. In the house on the moor where once stood the shack of the woman they called the Bone Crone, who once had a daughter they drowned in a stream. Who was buried under the coffin stone that sat on the edge of the Corpse Road.

And the stone was moved. And the earth stirred. And the Bone Crone rose again.

She is gone now. Has accomplished what she set out to do.

The destruction of something innocent.

David Lansdown waits in the bed, but he isn't alone.

He is tight against the form in the mattress beside him and thinks that just maybe, above the nauseating stench of water-bloated flesh, he can smell the boy with summer on his skin who was always afraid of what lurked in the dark.

Mary of the Moor

the truth behind the tale

The Bone Crone had not always been old, although most of the villagers in this tiny hamlet would beg to disagree. And the Bone Crone had not always been the Bone Crone.

That came after.

Once, there was a man. A soldier. Injured in a battle which killed most of his company, he had fallen upon her little house on the Corpse Road. Had, in fact, collapsed at her door as exhaustion and fever overcame him.

It was a wild night in October, and the wind howled over the barren moor, wailing like a banshee. Maybe it knew what was to come and was trying to warn her.

Compassion overcame the fear of a solitary man, and she took him into her tiny shack and laid him upon her bed of dried peat and old sackcloth. She drip-fed spoonfuls of thin gruel into his mouth and dressed his wounds as best she could with a salve of calendula and beeswax, made over the fire. And as she stirred, she muttered a healing spell to aid his recovery. A binding spell to keep him with her.

That was payment enough for saving his life.

He was a stockily built man with muscled shoulders. A straggly black beard flecked with grey hung from a prominent chin, and his eyes, when she pried them open, were a deep green like the forest.

The first night, she sat by his makeshift bed and watched as he writhed in pain, as the fever took him to the strange nightmare land between life and death. She mopped his brow with cool water, crooned sweet nothings against his ear.

Mary was not used to company. She had been abandoned by her own mother when she was but a babe, and it was only by the good grace from a parish priest that she had ever made it to adulthood.

'The Lord loves all,' he had told her, as she set about placing fresh flowers in the chipped pot vase by the church door. 'Even those such as you.'

He hadn't meant to be unkind, but she was a young girl and the words bit deep. The Lord may love her but no one else ever would. Not with her disfigurement.

And now she had a chance for the love she thought she would never have.

As the dawn light lit the rolling moor and she dozed beside him, the small fire an ember glow in the corner, her thoughts went to her future, and a giddiness she had never felt before fluttered in her stomach.

'What the hell!' His exclamation roused her from her slumber.

Her eyes flew open and met that dark green gaze. But all she saw in the forest depths was revulsion. 'Keep away from me.' His hand rose up as if to ward her off and to block her image from his eyes.

'You were hurt. I took you in,' she said. Instinctively, she retreated against the wall, away from the thin light sliding under the door.

A curse fell from his lips as he tried to sit up. Blood bloomed on the swaddling she had placed on his leg.

His mouth opened as though he was going to say something else, then a crease of pain furrowed his brow.

She stood, shivering like a reprimanded child, all of her dreams in ashes at her feet. He was just like all of the others, despite what she had done for him.

'I need to be on my feet,' he finally said. His voice carried a lilt. A man from the northern isles. 'Need to report back.'

Need to be away from here. From you. He didn't say it, but she heard it in the space between his words.

'You'll be needing to keep off that leg until the wound heals,' she replied. 'Or you'll be six feet under and reporting to the devil.'

His eyes flicked to hers as he raised himself up onto one elbow. 'What is this place?' For the first time it seemed to register where he was.

''Tis my home,' she said simply. Suddenly, she saw it through his eyes. The willow-weaved walls and roof, daubed with clay. The range, such as it was, with her single pan and kettle. Her only cup and plate. The dress she had washed in the stream the day before hanging from a bent twig in the corner.

A pauper's home. An outcast's sanctuary.

She moved a few steps closer. His lip curled upwards, disgust in his eyes.

Disappointment sang though her veins, and she wanted to laugh at her own rose-tinted dreams. Who was she to even think she could deserve happiness?

She stumbled back, her hand pushing the door open. Light danced in, eager to devour all shadow.

And then she was running over the moor, trampled heather under bare feet, tears streaking her dusty face. She ran until the stitch in her side made her collapse onto the sedge, her hands splayed on the ground. Fingers of early morning sun played on the bracken, turning the fronds to copper.

A plan hatched in her mind, but she recoiled from it.

Then, as her breathing settled, she saw what grew before her.

Carefully, she gathered the red pad-like leaves with glistening tendrils into her skirt. And as she did so, she found that a song had burst upon her lips.

Mary smiled. A smile of those who know the landscape on which they exist, and who never turn away from its offerings. It knew what she needed and was happy to oblige.

†

When she returned to her shack the door still stood open. Anticipation along with a nauseating soup of excitement and dread fermented in her stomach.

Part of her even hoped she would find her bed empty, her patient gone.

The stench of him met her nose first. Last night she had been too caught up in her ridiculous dream to notice it. But now, the stinking ripeness almost made her want to gag.

She found him half-propped up on the bed, his injured leg out in front of him. Blood mottled the entire surface of his bandages.

She inhaled sharply. There. The high, sweet scent of an embryonic rot.

A half-smile played on her lips.

'I've gathered some more herbs for your leg and to make a soup,' she said, as a way of greeting. 'Maybe by tomorrow you can be on your way. I know a man who may be able to lend you a horse.'

She dangled this visual carrot before him, saw his eyes greedily devour it and the thought of freedom.

Without another word she busied herself, boiling water and stripping the plant into portions, separating the stem and root and leaf. She could feel his eyes upon her as she worked but paid him no heed.

As she waited for the potion to thicken, she heard his throat working. He spat a large green wad of phlegm onto the ground. 'What's your name, wench?'

She pulled an old milking stool from the corner and settled herself upon it, her skirts dangling between her legs.

'They call me Mary.' The name felt alien on her tongue, as none used it to address her. It was the name the priest had given her. A biblical name, as though it could save her soul.

She could feel him studying her face as she deftly unwound the blood-sodden bandages. Could feel him lingering on the misshapen socket with her sightless eye.

She hung her head lower, letting her long brown hair obscure his view.

'Thomas.' He offered his own name into the silence.

It was a good name, and inside her heart she wept.

The wound had closed a little but it was slightly swollen at the edges, and that high, sweet smell seemed to almost pulse in time with his heartbeat. She applied more of the salve and he did not complain, but she saw his fingers tighten on the edges of the bed.

'I need leeches,' he said, watching as she wrapped fresh padding around his leg.

'There's a village not far,' she said, 'at the base of the moor. About half a day's walk. You can try there.'

She noted that he seemed to *need* everything.

When the broth was ready he drank it greedily, slurping the remnants from the wooden bowl. It didn't take long for his eyes to glaze over. He lay down on the makeshift bed and she went to sit beside him. A chuckle came from his throat. His hand flopped languidly over hers.

'Bring a man some ale, wench.'

She smiled to herself. The toxins in the roots she had brewed were working their magic. He would no longer see her as something to be pitied, something to shy away from.

She scooped another ladle of the watery broth and poured it into a cup made from a hollow sheep skull. He drank it down, the liquid spilling from the sides of his mouth.

Minutes passed, where he mumbled and talked to invisible people.

Now she could take her chance.

His stained breeches were held together with rope and departed his body easily. She lifted her skirts and straddled him, rubbing herself against his limp member.

In seconds it was limp no more and she took him into her body, an incantation on her lips as she rode him without mercy.

The sound of his release seemed to shake the rafters of her little house, and as she lay down beside him, as he drifted into a dreamless sleep, she wished for his seed to take root.

He slept all through the day and all through the night, waking at dawn and demanding she bring him his boots. She did all that he asked for, a demure and willing soul, even gifting him with a stout crook she had fashioned out of a windfall branch from the blackthorn tree outside her door to aid his walking.

And as he limped down the hill towards the small holding she had directed him to, where he would find the owner none too pleased to see him, she smiled, her hand coming to rest on her belly.

†

Nine months later, after a long and arduous labour, she delivered herself of a squalling red-faced babe. A girl-child who grew to be pretty, who spent her days running barefoot on the moor.

But she carried an affliction, all of her fingers webbed together. When they went down to the market the boys threw lumps of pond weed at them and made mocking quacking noises. The cruelty of the young has a special kind of barb.

So Mary of the Moor took to going to market by herself. The taunts and jeers still came, but she could weather them.

Back then she was too naïve, content to live and let live despite her ill-treatment.

But now, even long dead, the fire from that day still scorched her veins, the woman she had been reduced to ash.

She forced herself to relive it, to open up the scabs which pocked her heart. *Let it bleed*, she whispered. *Let it bleed and let me remember.*

†

It happened on May Day.

The sky over the moor was cornflower blue and a warm breeze danced across the sedge. Bees droned around the heather, and Mary of the Moor watched her daughter playing on the river bank.

'I will be gone near the full day,' Mary said, as she hefted the sack containing pockets of herbal remedies to sell at market onto her back. 'If you see a stranger, what are you to do?'

Amabel stopped her stacking of stones by the river's edge. 'I am to go inside,' she said, 'for strangers are to be feared.'

Mary grunted and set off down the dusty track—*the Corpse Road*—leading to the village. The celebrations would bring more travellers, and she could not risk Amabel falling prey to any that might pass her shack on their way.

The village was awash with people, but she kept her head down until she reached the spot just beyond the well where she set down her sack. From here she could see the frivolities, but she was not part of them. Children raced past her, laughing and jostling each other, flower crowns in their hair.

A pang of regret wrenched her heart. How Amabel would have loved to take part.

She held out a few pockets of herbs to a passing couple.

'For your ailments, m'lady,' she offered.

The woman brought the back of her hand to her nose. Her companion swept the pocket from Mary's fingers. It landed in the dust, the precious dried herbs spilling out.

'Be off with you, Mary of the Moor. Your like is not welcome here.'

She shrank back, kept her gaze lowered, their unkindness a sting against her heart.

Fiddle music drifted across from the village green. People quickened their steps towards it. Mary could see the tall sapling through gaps in the crowd.

Garlands of leaves and flowers bedecked it. The children were gathered at its base, their hands clasped.

The sun rose high in the sky and her lips grew dry. She looked longingly at the well, but no one offered her a cup from the bucket as they passed.

As the revelry rose to its peak she was, at last, given a moment to take a sip. She clasped the wooden cup between her palms but as she brought it to her lips it was not the reflection of her face she saw.

It was Amabel, her mouth open in a silent scream.

Mary felt her heart lurch. She stumbled to a man tending to his horse at a watering trough.

'Please sir,' she begged, 'can you take me home? I am afeared for my daughter's safety.'

He shoved her away with his shoulder and she fell in the dust. 'Leave me be, hag.' A wad of spittle landed on her cheek.

She clambered to her feet, panic coursing through her veins. There was no one here who would help her.

So she did the only thing she could. She made her way back up the dusty track, over the moor in the blinding sunlight, back to the place where she knew heartbreak was waiting.

There was silence in the dark of the shack. Silence on the moor as she staggered down to the river. She called her daughter's name, wading through the shallows of the water, her soaked skirts heavy around her ankles.

It was only as she rounded the bend of the river, as it meandered past the large outcrop of rock locals called the Devil's Fist, that she heard her daughter's scream.

Raucous laughter followed. The sound of displaced water.

Two men held Amabel in their grasp. One had his knee upon her daughter's back and the other his hand tangled in her hair.

'See how the frog wench sings.'

'Duck her under again, Pie, I likes to see her squirm.'

Mary watched in horror as Amabel's face was shoved under the surface of the water.

'Stop!' she cried, although she knew they would not. She tried to run, but her skirts dragged her down.

Amabel fought back as much as she was able, but she was tiring and each time they ducked her head under her struggles became weaker.

Mary prayed to all her goddesses for the life of her daughter, but they, too, did not listen. And when she finally came to Amabel's side, her daughter lay facedown in the shallows, her dark hair floating like weed in the quiet current.

The men stood by the river's edge a little way ahead. One had pulled a stalk of moor grass from a tuft and was sucking its edge.

She did not remember the curses she hurled at them, but she remembered the agony of loss as it clawed through her flesh, the thirst in her soul for retribution.

She sank into the water and cradled her daughter in her arms.

High above, in the cloudless sky, Mary heard a crow's plaintive cry. Through tear-filled eyes she cast her gaze towards the heavens and saw others join the single bird, wheeling and diving together until they formed a black mass that drowned out the sun.

She buried Amabel in the shade of the blackthorn tree which stood by her shack. A place her daughter had sat and played. A place she had loved when the blossom drifted down, covering her dark hair with snow petals.

And whatever the weather, she would walk in the same shallows in which her daughter had perished. In time, the river and the Bone Crone—for Mary of the

Moor died on that day with her daughter—came to an agreement.

The Bone Crone did not go down to the village again. But it had naught to do with the fact she had been banished. She waited and she schemed and she made her deals with the devils who visited her in the dead of night. Something innocent had been ripped from her. And she would make those who came after pay the same price.

Crops failed. Babes died. Villager fought villager.

The village fell to plague in the year 1666.

That was not her doing, but she did not mourn those who died.

And when she, too, met her maker, they buried her body under the heaviest stone they could find, lest she rise again.

Did you enjoy this book?
You can make a big difference.

When it comes to getting attention for my books, reviews are the most powerful tools. Much as I'd like to take out full page advertisements or put posters on buses, I don't have the financial muscle of a big publisher.

But I do have something those publishers would love to get their hands on.

A committed and loyal group of readers.

Honest reviews of my books help bring them to the attention of other readers and helps me to continue to create stories for you to fall in love with. If you've enjoyed reading this book I would be very grateful if you could leave a review (it can be as short as you like).

Acknowledgements

A book starts with the writer, but there are so many other people who nurture it through its growth from seed to flower. This is my first novella but it started out as a novel. At 57k I realised it wasn't working. I'd lost the core, the beating heart. I had to strip it back to what was important—Luca and David's story. So this little book bears many scars in its creation but I hope it is stronger for them. Without my support crew, I'm quite sure I would have lost the last of my sanity. My grateful thanks to my wonderful editor, Rae Oestreich, who took this from an early draft and who helped shape it into the story in your hands. My beta readers who received an early draft of this and waded through with comments and suggestions – Ross Jeffery, G.R. Thomas, Alyson Faye, Becky Wright, Josh Radwell, and Lisa Niblock. And to Sarina Langer, Lydia Koster and Shane Douglas Keene for that all important first critique. To Kealan Patrick Burke and Elderlemon Design for my haunting cover creation. To Platform House Publishing for beautiful interior design. You are all absolute stars.

Thank you to my friends and loyal supporters on Twitter and the #bookstagram community on Instagram, for showing me the human side of social media. Writing is a solitary craft but I am never alone with your constant loyalty and encouragement.

And to those who discover my books through other sources—welcome, and my warmest thanks.

About the author

Beverley Lee is the bestselling author of the Gabriel Davenport vampire suspense series *(The Making of Gabriel Davenport, A Shining in the Shadows and The Purity of Crimson)* and the grief/gothic horror, *The Ruin of Delicate Things*. Her shorter fiction has been included in works from Cemetery Gates Media, Kandisha Press and Off Limits Press. In thrall to the written word from an early age, especially the darker side of fiction, she believes that the very best story is the one you have to tell. Supporting fellow authors is also her passion and she is actively involved in social media and writers' groups.

You can visit her online at www.beverleylee.com (where you'll find a free dark and twisted short story download) or on Instagram (@theconstantvoice) and Twitter (@constantvoice).

Printed in Great Britain
by Amazon